# Stefania Hartley

ALSO AVAILABLE AS EBOOK AND LARGE PRINT

Copyright © 2025 Stefania Hartley

ISBN: 978-1-914606-62-5

Stefania Hartley asserts the moral right to be identified as the author of this work.

This is a work of fiction. Names, characters and events are solely the product of the author's imagination.

Stories 1 to 15 and 17 to 31 were first published in The People's Friend magazine.

Edited by Sandy Salisbury
Cover illustration and design by Joseph Witchall
https://josephwitchall.com/

# CONTENTS

| | | |
|---|---|---|
| 1 | Obedience | 1 |
| 2 | A Feminine Touch | 5 |
| 3 | Pin Up | 9 |
| 4 | The Holy Spirit of Competition | 13 |
| 5 | A Spruce Up | 17 |
| 6 | The Good Shepherds | 21 |
| 7 | The Vow of Patience | 25 |
| 8 | The Wheels on The Bus | 29 |
| 9 | New Year Surprise | 33 |
| 10 | Rethink The Sink | 37 |
| 11 | Stitch Them Up! | 41 |
| 12 | Dressing Down | 45 |
| 13 | Chains of Events | 49 |
| 14 | The Bishop's Visit | 53 |
| 15 | The Best Valentine's Day | 57 |
| 16 | Testing Times | 61 |

| | | |
|---|---|---|
| 17 | Birthday Twins | 66 |
| 18 | The Carnival Parade | 70 |
| 19 | Fasting | 74 |
| 20 | Agony Aunt | 78 |
| 21 | Pigsty | 82 |
| 22 | Nun of The Year | 86 |
| 23 | The Average Nun | 90 |
| 24 | In Debt | 94 |
| 25 | An Unexpected Bonus | 98 |
| 26 | Sangria | 102 |
| 27 | Sanremo | 106 |
| 28 | Mother's Hen | 109 |
| 29 | Parting Gifts | 114 |
| 30 | Give Me Peace | 118 |
| 31 | Shepherdesses | 122 |
| | Other Books by the Author | 126 |
| | About the Author | 135 |

## 1. OBEDIENCE

Hens weren't as obedient as nuns, Sister Luce thought as she tried to coax the birds out of their coop for their morning feed.

"Come on. Don't be shy," she told them.

She knew a lot about shyness. Thankfully she was only shy with people, not with animals or God. So life in the convent of Santa Maria Silvana, in the Italian Apennine mountains, surrounded by swathes of forests and wildlife, was just right for her.

A life of prayer and quiet work in the service of God and neighbour was all she'd ever wanted, and she had entered it as soon as she had completed her studies, only three years before. This made her the most junior nun in the convent, which suited her very well. Leadership and responsibilities brought attention, and she hated attention.

Even managing the convent's chicken flock was one leadership role too many for Sister

Luce but, on entering the convent, she had taken the vows of poverty, chastity and obedience. So when the Mother Superior had asked her to be in charge of the chickens, Sister Luce had said yes.

Despite these responsibilities and anxieties, Sister Luce was contented with her life and wouldn't have changed a thing.

Which was why she was apprehensive about the meeting the Mother Superior had called for that afternoon. Were there changes afoot?

When the bells summoned the nuns scattered throughout fields, orchards, pens and workshops, Sister Luce took off her apron, washed her hands and headed back.

With rustling of habits and clacking of sandals, all the convent's twenty-two sisters gathered in the meeting room, eager to hear Mother Speranza's announcement.

"I'm sure you are all aware of the misconceptions about convent life that circulate out in the world," she began. "Some people imagine nuns as embittered, disillusioned people who hate the world."

Heads nodded.

"Wouldn't it be nice if we could show the world how happy and fulfilled we are? Other women might even discover that they want this life too."

Heads nodded again.

"How can we do that? We can't let everybody into the convent," Sister Gioconda, the porter, asked.

"We won't need to." Mother Speranza smiled. "I've just been approached by a TV producer who would like to make a documentary about convent life. If we let their crew into our home, they will bring us into people's homes."

A mixture of excitement and apprehension rippled through the room. Meanwhile, Sister Luce shrank against her chair. Talking to one person was stressful enough; talking to millions through a camera didn't bear thinking about.

"I don't have any details yet," Mother Speranza declared, "but there's one thing we've been asked to decide. We need to pick who will chaperone the crew and be the 'poster nun' for our convent."

"You, Mother," someone called out.

"It should be someone younger, so young viewers can relate better," Mother Speranza replied.

Sister Luce tried to hide behind her veil, but the Mother Superior was looking at her.

"Sister Luce would be perfect," she suggested, and everyone agreed.

Sister Luce couldn't think of any reason to

refuse other than that it would be unpleasant and terrifying for her. But if she only did pleasant and easy things, what virtue would there be in that? Surely obedience was a vow because it didn't come easy. So she said yes and the other nuns thanked her and congratulated her.

When Sister Luce returned to her hens that evening, her steps lacked their usual bounce.

"I'm terrified of standing in front of a camera," she confided to the birds.

In the light of the autumn sunset, their feathers gleamed like amber. The convent's honey-coloured stones, too, glowed golden in the sunset, and the forest was a riot of yellows, oranges and reds.

A thought comforted her. Maybe the film crew weren't going to pay much attention to a nun in a drab habit when everything else was so much more photogenic. She could only hope.

## 2. A FEMININE TOUCH

When Sister Luce had taken the vows of poverty, chastity and obedience, she hadn't imagined that obedience would be the hardest to keep.

It was only out of obedience that she had accepted the job of accompanying the TV crew who would be coming to film a documentary about convent life.

"I'll be away for a few days to meet the TV producer," Mother Speranza told her. "Could you give the convent a spruce up while I'm gone? Feel free to ask the other sisters for help."

Sister Luce would have been very happy to help make the convent as photogenic as possible—the more beautiful the convent, the more chances the TV cameras would be focusing on it rather than her. But Mother Speranza was putting her in charge of the spruce-up, and Sister Luce hated being in charge. Even being in charge of the convent's flock of hens was a responsibility that caused her anxiety.

But there was that vow of obedience again, and she didn't want to say no.

"Yes, Mother," she said, then rushed to the chapel and prayed for divine help.

Just as she was leaving the chapel, help arrived in the form of Sister Benedetta.

"Mother Speranza told me that you're going to give the convent a makeover. I'm very happy to help," the nun said. She was in charge of the woodworking workshop and general repairs.

Sister Luce accepted the offer.

"We should start from the entrance and make our way in as if we were the TV crew on their arrival," Sister Benedetta suggested, and Sister Luce agreed.

The first thing they noticed was some paint peeling off the walls in the corridor.

"A lick of paint will do wonders. I just happen to have some leftover wall paint in my workshop," Sister Benedetta said.

It sounded like a good plan, until Sister Luce saw the cans of paint.

"I'm not sure about the colour. Shouldn't we replace like with like?" she ventured.

"Not at all: a makeover requires change."

Sister Luce still wasn't sure about changing

the colour scheme, but she was swept in by Sister Benedetta's enthusiasm. Two days later, not only the corridor but two other rooms had had a new coat of paint.

Next they inspected the refectory. Sister Benedetta fixed any stools and tables with wobbly legs and crafted some extra stools, in case the TV people wished to stay for lunch. Sister Luce was pleased with their work.

But then Sister Benedetta came up with the idea of making cushions for the stools and got the seamstress nuns involved. They insisted that lace doilies on the dining tables were also necessary. It took all of Sister Luce's powers of persuasion to make them give up on the doilies, but in return she agreed that they could decorate the ropes of the convent's bells with ribbons and sprigs of lavender.

No sooner had they finished than Mother Speranza drove through the gates.

Faced with the corridor in front of her—now the same colour of pink candyfloss—her eyebrows shot up.

She stared at the bells' ropes transformed into maypoles and her eyes widened at the sight of the refectory's pink gingham cushions, tablecloths and curtains.

Sister Luce shrank inside her habit. She should have been more assertive when she'd disagreed with the changes.

"Do you like what we've done, Mother?" Sister Benedetta asked with a grin.

"It's not quite what I was expecting," the Mother said diplomatically. "Our order's colour palette is brown."

"Yes, but St Francis chose it because it was the colour of poor people's clothes back when dyes were expensive and the poor could only afford undyed wool. But now that there are cheap synthetic dyes, it makes no difference. And pink is a celebration of our femininity," Sister Benedetta added.

"I have no objections to pink," Mother Speranza said with a smile. "I just wasn't expecting it. But I like what you've done and I like pink too. In fact, it's my favourite colour." Her eyes heavenward, Sister Luce let out a breath of relief.

## 3. PIN UP

During the convent's pink makeover, Sister Luce had noticed that the sewing workshop was in a terrible mess. There were cloths piled on chairs, cotton reels rolling on the floor and pin cushions everywhere.

After some fervent praying, Sister Luce gathered the courage to approach Sister Teodora, the formidable eighty-seven-year-old nun in charge of the workshop.

Sister Teodora was embroidering an altar tablecloth surrounded by piles of white cloth so high around her that she looked like an angel on a cloud.

It took several attempts before Sister Teodora understood the reason of Sister Luce's visit.

"I've got used to where things are and, with my poor memory, if I move anything, I will struggle to find it," she replied. "And Sister Maddalena's eyesight isn't great, so she needs everything to stay where it is."

"I'm all in favour of a tidy-up, especially if it makes it easier for us to move around," Sister Maddalena called out from her workstation.

Her eyesight might be poor, but her hearing was excellent.

But Sister Teodora was still reluctant.

"The TV people won't be able to come in with cameras and microphones if the floor is cluttered," Sister Maddalena persisted.

"That won't do. We must be able to show off our creations!" Sister Teodora agreed.

Sister Teodora didn't trust other nuns to help them except Sister Luce, who found herself carrying around bolts of fabric, sewing machines and boxes all day long.

Luckily cabinets and drawers were empty, so there was plenty of space to tidy things away.

Sister Luce then wrote the contents of every drawer in large letters on labels so that the seamstresses could find their things without having to resort to memory.

After two days of work, the workshop was finally clear of clutter and the room looked a lot more spacious than before. Light could stream through the windows unimpeded, making it easier for Sister Maddalena's eyes. Now even the most cumbersome of cameras and boom microphones could easily move around.

"A pin cushion is missing," Sister Teodora announced.

"Are you sure?" Sister Luce asked. There had been so many scattered around.

"Yes. We've always had twelve, like the apostles."

"Maybe the missing one is Judah?" Sister Luce joked, but Sister Teodora didn't smile.

"You wouldn't like it if even one pin ended up on your chair or in your bed, or in your soup."

The hunt for the missing pin cushion started at once. Drawers were opened, cabinets emptied, boxes moved, and soon the room was messy again.

The three nuns were so engrossed in the job that they didn't hear the bells calling them to prayer in the chapel.

"Are you okay? We are all waiting for you to start the evening prayer," the Mother Superior said, walking into the workshop.

She looked around and Sister Luce's heart squeezed. If only Mother Speranza had come in earlier, when they still had a tidy room to show off…

Now, the room was a mess and the three of them were in disgrace for holding up the evening prayer.

They followed the Mother to the chapel, where all the other nuns were already in their pews. Sister Luce was scuttling towards her usual pew when a metallic glint in the Mother's habit caught her eye.

Clinging to a fold of her skirt was a small pin cushion! It must have stuck to her habit when she'd come into the workshop.

Just as Mother Speranza was about to sit down, Sister Luce leapt forward and snatched the porcupine off her skirt.

After a moment of stunned silence, everyone gasped when they realised what had happened.

"Thank you, Sister Luce. You've saved me from a painful experience," the Mother Superior said, and her smile of gratitude told Sister Luce that she wasn't in disgrace anymore.

Tomorrow they would tidy up the workshop again, but for tonight everyone was happy.

## 4. THE HOLY SPIRIT OF COMPETITION

Since Mother Superior had agreed to open the convent's doors to a documentary crew, life in the Convento di Maria Silvana had not been the same.

Sister Luce had worked hard to spruce up the communal spaces, and Mother Speranza had congratulated her on her work.

"We want to show viewers that our lives are fulfilled and happy," Mother Speranza told her nuns.

"We should take the TV crew on a tractor tour of the vineyard," Sister Deodata proposed.

She looked after the vineyard and loved racing up and down the rows of vines on the tractor.

"They should visit our sewing workshop," Sister Maddalena suggested.

After the chapel, the sewing workshop was her happiest place.

Sister Luce thought the film crew should come and see her hens—her pride and joy—but she was too shy to speak up.

"These are all good suggestions," Mother Speranza said, "but we don't want viewers to think that nuns only work and never play. I've decided to invite the TV crew to film our relaxation hour."

Every afternoon, between three and four, the nuns enjoyed one hour of communal rest and relaxation. In good weather they gathered in the garden, where the more athletic nuns played ball on the grass while others chatted on the benches in the sun. Sister Luce always sat on the bench to crochet and chat with the older nuns.

"We'll rehearse it this afternoon," Mother Speranza added.

Sister Luce wondered what aspect of rest and relaxation could need rehearsing, but she trusted Mother Superior knew what to do.

That afternoon, a gentle sun shone on the garden and the temperature was pleasant, but everyone was on edge.

"Do we have a script? Lines to learn?" Sister Deodata asked.

"There's no script," Mother Speranza told

them. "The producer has stressed that we must behave naturally. But our usual ball games aren't very exciting, and we don't want people to think that nuns are boring. I thought we could play other games, like 'Steal the Flag'," Mother Speranza added, and pulled a clean handkerchief—the flag—out of her pocket.

Sister Luce sank back into her bench.

The sisters who hadn't grown up in Italy didn't know the traditional Italian playground game and needed to have it explained. Two teams were formed and each member was given a number.

When Mother Speranza called a number, the sister with that number in each team had to run and grab the handkerchief from Mother Speranza's hand before their opponent and bring it back to their team without being tagged by their adversary.

"Three!" Mother Speranza called.

Sisters Grazia and Angelica sprinted off. Sister Grazia got the handkerchief, but Sister Angelica rugby-tackled her to the ground.

"A tap on the shoulder will suffice," Mother Speranza reminded everyone.

At the next round, Sister Deodata got the handkerchief, but Sister Benedetta ran after her, and her "tap on the shoulder" made Sister Deodata lose her veil.

"I think we ought to play a calmer game," Mother Speranza said.

Someone suggested hide-and-seek, but it was agreed that it would be too hard for the TV crew to film it.

When it looked impossible to reach a consensus, Mother Speranza sighed. "I give up on organising games. Play whatever you want." She wiped her brow with the handkerchief and stuffed it into her pocket.

Someone retrieved the ball and a game started.

Mother Speranza sat down on the bench between Sister Luce and Sister Gioconda's wheelchair.

As she watched the sisters pass the ball to each other, she confided to the other two. "I can't understand what they like about this game. There seem to be no rules."

"Perhaps convent life already has enough rules." Sister Gioconda smiled.

## 5. A SPRUCE UP

Sister Luce looked out of her window to the forest that stretched over the Apennines. She had spent weeks sprucing up the convent for the TV crew's arrival and now she longed to be outdoors.

She'd love to have an excuse to go on a hike in the spruce forest. An idea came to her: she could go on a recce of the forest to find the most scenic spots to take the TV crew.

She pitched the idea to Mother Speranza, who was enthusiastic about it.

"Our convent is dedicated to Mother Mary of the Forests so it would be appropriate to feature the forest in the documentary. Start with a visit to our chestnut grove. Sister Silvestra is in charge of the grove and will be happy to answer any questions."

Visiting the chestnut grove around the convent wasn't the hike in the wilderness that Sister Luce had imagined, but it would still be outdoors. And perhaps, on the way back, she might take a detour into the spruce forest.

\*\*\*

Sister Silvestra was very excited to take Sister Luce on a tour of the chestnut grove.

"The chestnuts have seen the locals through many winters. Some varieties are nice to eat fresh—roasted or boiled. Others are best turned into flour to make polenta, bread and cakes," Sister Silvestra explained.

Having grown up in warmer parts of Italy, the only chestnuts Sister Luce had known were roasted ones sold by street vendors.

They reached a stone building where the recently harvested chestnuts were being dried on a wooden loft over a slow fire.

"It'll burn for thirty days," Sister Silvestra explained. "Then the dried chestnuts go through a machine to remove the husks. They'll be toasted, then ground into flour."

Sister Silvestra showed Sister Luce to her workshop, where some *castagnaccio* cakes were ready to come out of the oven. Just then, Sister Grazia arrived to collect some cakes for the pilgrims' guesthouse.

"You both should try a slice!" Sister Silvestra suggested, and the two sisters accepted eagerly.

Sister Grazia had recently joined from the Philippines, and Sister Silvestra spent most of her time in the chestnut grove, so it was nice getting to know them both better.

"Are you looking forward to the documentary?" Sister Grazia asked.

"I can't wait to talk about all the wonderful things the humble chestnut gives us," Sister Silvestra said.

Sister Luce lowered her gaze. "I'm not looking forward to the documentary at all. I'm very shy and I struggle to talk to strangers."

Both sisters reassured Sister Luce that it was okay to be shy.

By the time the bell called everyone back for the evening prayer, it was getting dark. Sister Luce had missed her chance to go in the spruce forest, but it had been worth it.

While Sister Silvestra locked up, Sister Luce and Sister Grazia went ahead.

The convent wasn't far but the chestnut grove was now shrouded in the evening's darkness and Sister Grazia grew very quiet.

"Are there bears in these mountains?" she asked.

"Yes, but few are left. The Marsican brown bear is endangered," Sister Luce replied.

"What about wolves and wild boars?"

"Those are a lot more common," Sister Luce said cheerfully.

Sister Grazia glanced nervously over her

shoulders. Sister Luce realised that her companion was frightened of wild animals.

"But they've never been known to attack a nun—especially not a Franciscan one," Sister Luce said to reassure her.

Once they were safely back indoors, Sister Grazia turned to Sister Luce with a grateful smile. "Thank you for walking back with me. You are so brave."

Sister Luce had never considered herself brave, but there clearly were different kinds of bravery.

That night, as she looked out of her window to the forest she still hadn't managed to visit, Sister Luce thought about the documentary.

She still dreaded it, but today she had discovered a silver lining. Thanks to the documentary, she was getting to know her fellow sisters better.

## 6. THE GOOD SHEPHERD

It was a sunny day and Sister Luce thought about the forest hike she still hadn't managed to do. Would today be the day?

When Mother Speranza called her into her office, she knew it wouldn't be. The Mother Superior was bound to give her some job around the convent.

"I'd like you to liaise with Sister Angelica to ensure our chapel is looking its best for the documentary," Mother Speranza said.

So Sister Luce had to give up her hike plans and head to the chapel instead.

Sister Angelica was older than Sister Luce, but just as quiet and shy. When Mother Speranza had assigned her to the care of the chapel, Sister Angelica had found her happiest place.

She kept all the books, vessels, candles and vestments in perfect order, and her flower arrangements were spectacular.

But when Sister Luce informed her of the Mother's request, Sister Angelica was thrown into a panic. "I don't know where to start!"

"We need fresh flower arrangements," Sister Luce reassured her. "Our convent is dedicated to Mother Mary of the Forests, so how about a woodland theme?"

"Good idea."

Then Sister Luce had another idea—one that would give her the much-desired hike in the forest. "We could go and collect greeneries from the woods now."

Sister Angelica thought it was a splendid idea. They took baskets and secateurs and they set off to collect green ferns, fir, ivy and brightly coloured berries, until their baskets were overflowing.

"I'm sure we've passed this rock," Sister Angelica said when they'd walked for a while.

The clouds had covered the sun so the two nuns couldn't tell if they were going east or west.

"I'll check my phone," Sister Luce said, but there was no phone reception.

They continued walking but, when they passed the same rock for a third time, Sister Luce had to agree that they were lost.

Guilt and regrets assailed her. She should have shared their planned route with the convent and taken a map and a compass. Above all, she regretted inviting another sister to perish in the woods with her.

They sat on the now very familiar rock and prayed more fervently than ever. A roof for the night, a bed and a meal—things they had taken for granted—now seemed an unobtainable dream.

"We could build a shelter with branches and moss," Sister Luce suggested.

Suddenly they heard animal noises.

"We'll be devoured by wolves! Martyred for the chapel!" Sister Angelica cried.

"It's not howling. It's neighing," Sister Luce told her.

A convoy of horses appeared on a path. The herdsmen were as surprised to meet the two nuns as they were to meet them.

"God must have sent you!" Sister Angelica exclaimed.

The herdsmen, who were taking their horses from the high-altitude summer pastures down to the valley for winter, offered the stranded nuns a lift to the convent on horseback.

Despite having never ridden before, Sister Luce and Sister Angelica readily agreed. They were given the most placid horses and the most comfortable saddles, and the convoy detoured to the convent.

When the missing sisters entered the convent with their equestrian cortège, everyone was surprised and relieved.

Mother Speranza treated the kind herdsmen to a hearty warm supper and a comfy bed in the pilgrims' guesthouse. The horses were given water, hay and a shelter in the convent's old stables.

During the evening prayers in the chapel, Sister Luce thanked God for their safe return home and also for the hike and the bonus horseback ride.

She had now had her fill of the great outdoors and looked forward to spending the coming days working quietly within the safety of the convent's walls.

But Mother Speranza had something else in store for her the next morning.

"Your trip to the forest gave me an idea," she told Sister Luce. "Could you pop to the lake over the mountain and look for good filming spots?"

## 7. THE VOW OF PATIENCE

The day had arrived for the film crew to visit the convent. Mother Speranza introduced the producer and director, Alessia, and the camerawoman, Leonia, to all the sisters gathered in the meeting room.

Sister Luce was relieved to find that they were just ordinary women and not the scary monsters she had imagined.

Sister Luce and Mother Speranza took them on a tour of the convent.

"Where are your Christmas decorations?" Alessia asked after a while. "I was planning to start the documentary with a Christmas feel."

"Advent doesn't start until tomorrow," Mother Speranza explained. "There will be signs of Christmas all over the convent from tomorrow."

"Shall we come back tomorrow?" Alessia asked.

"We don't work on a Sunday."

Alessia reluctantly agreed to return on Monday.

For the rest of that day, Sister Luce, Sister Benedetta and Sister Grazia put together the nativity scene in the chapel. Sister Luce felt quite proud of their job, and Mother Speranza congratulated them.

When Monday arrived, Alessia and Leonia surveyed the place with a disappointed expression.

"Where is your tree?" Alessia asked.

"There are plenty of trees in the woods outside," Mother Speranza explained.

"What about the twinkling of fairy lights, the shine of baubles, the sparkle of tinsel?"

"We've made a vow of poverty."

"This is going to change all our plans..." Alessia looked stricken.

"Why don't we discuss these plans with a cup of coffee?" the Mother Superior suggested kindly.

Everyone agreed that it was a good idea and they followed her, while Sister Luce went to the kitchen to make their coffees. The situation required some cake, so she cut four generous slices of chestnut cake.

After the coffee and the cake, everyone looked more relaxed.

"So what do you have in mind?" Mother

Speranza asked the producer.

"I want the documentary to start with some Christmas magic. I thought a convent, where nuns pray to Jesus all the time, must be the best place to find that lovely Christmassy feeling…" Alessia turned to Leonia for help.

"That warmth and cosiness that makes you feel loved," Leonia added.

"I see." Mother Speranza nodded. "Then we might just have what you want."

Mother Speranza led the way to the chapel, where Alessia and Leonia looked at the nativity scene with dismay.

"It's just a pile of twigs and moss!" Alessia cried.

"There are clay figurines. We made them ourselves," Sister Luce said protectively.

She and Sister Benedetta had put together that scene with great care. They'd sourced four kinds of moss to render the various crops in the fields and real twigs for the manger and the fire. Sister Luce was proud of their nativity's sylvan vibes and had even thought it might be trendy.

Alessia pointed at the empty manger with an exasperated gesture. "There's not even a Baby Jesus!"

"It's not Christmas yet," Mother Speranza pointed out, and Alessia sighed.

"You nuns must have taken the vow of patience on top of all those others."

Sister Luce thought that a vow of patience would be a very good idea. Right now, though, she wanted to help Alessia, who looked like she was on the verge of breaking down.

Suddenly Mother Speranza's face lit up. "If Baby Jesus is what you're looking for, come with me."

They all followed the Mother Superior to her cell. In the privacy of her room, on a windowsill facing the Apennine forests stretching to the horizon, sat a little basket containing a tiny hand-knitted woollen blanket. And tucked in that blanket lay the cutest, chubbiest Baby Jesus Sister Luce had ever seen. It radiated warmth, hope and contentment.

"Yes! This is it!" Alessia cried in triumph. "We'll start the documentary here!"

## 8. THE WHEELS ON THE BUS

Mother Speranza urged the producer and the camerawoman to spend Christmas Day with their families, but they refused, explaining that they wanted to capture the convent's "Christmas vibes".

This meant that, first thing on Christmas morning, Sister Luce's hopes for a quiet Christmas were dashed at the sight of Alessia and Leonia's car trundling up the mountain.

"Every Christmas Day some sisters bring presents to the homeless shelter in town," Mother Speranza told Alessia, suggesting she filmed them.

"The shelter is a dreary place. Not at all Christmassy," Alessia protested.

Sister Luce had to agree that the squat, grey building wasn't pretty, but Mother Speranza couldn't see how giving presents to the poor wasn't Christmassy enough.

After some discussion, it was agreed that the sisters' car would be decorated with fairy lights and the sisters would be wearing tinsel crowns.

The enormous bag of gifts took so much space that only four sisters could fit in the car. Mother Speranza chose Sister Luce, Sister Grazia, Sister Angelica, because she rarely left the convent, and Sister Benedetta, being the only one who could make their car behave.

Leonia filmed the four of them as they squeezed into their battered old car and were waved off by the other sisters.

Alessia and Leonia followed them in their own car down the mountain's hairpin bends.

In the absence of a car stereo, the young nuns entertained themselves singing songs. They were half-way through "The Wheels on The Bus" when the car joined in with an ominous rattle.

A few metres later, the car slowed to a stop and wouldn't start again. Sister Benedetta looked under the smoking bonnet and declared that, this time, she couldn't fix it.

Unfortunately, Alessia and Leonia's car was stuffed with filming equipment, leaving only enough space for the bag of gifts.

"Don't you have any breakdown cover?" Alessia asked.

"Our breakdown cover is the divine providence," Sister Luce replied.

As Sister Benedetta held out her thumb to

hitch a ride, the others began to pray.

Alessia rang for a taxi, but those working on Christmas Day were all booked up and none of the cars that drove past had four empty seats.

Time ticked on, the sisters were late for their appointment and the roads were emptying out as people were having their Christmas lunch.

A car appeared in the distance and the sisters prayed that it would stop for them. As it approached at tremendous speed, they prayed instead that it wouldn't mow them down.

With a screeching of tyres, the car stopped in front of them. It had four empty seats and one driver—Santa Claus.

The producer's face lit up. "The stranded nuns get a lift from Saint Nicholas!" she announced excitedly to the camera.

The young man in a plastic beard was more than happy to offer the sisters a lift because he, too, was headed to the homeless shelter and was running late. On his first time in the role, the young Santa Claus had grossly underestimated the time required for fixing his beard and moustache into place. He hoped that, by rescuing the nuns, he would be excused for his lateness.

The four nuns piled into the car and sped off with Alessia and Leonia in hot pursuit, filming all the time.

When Santa Claus and the nuns finally reached the shelter with their bags of goodies, volunteers and guests rejoiced.

Back at the convent, someone wasn't in the mood for rejoicing. Mother Speranza had organised for a garage to pick up the car and determine if it was salvageable. If the convent needed a new car, the money from the documentary would be sorely needed.

"How did the filming go?" Mother Speranza asked Alessia when everyone returned. "Did you manage to capture what you were looking for?"

"No," Alessia replied with a smile. "What we got is a lot better."

## 9. NEW YEAR SURPRISE

"Alessia wants to film on New Year's Eve," Mother Speranza told Sister Luce.

"There won't be much to film. We always go to bed after night prayers," Sister Luce pointed out.

"I could refuse but I don't want to displease her again. Also, we really need the money from this documentary now that we have to replace our car."

"Could we buy a minibus?" Sister Luce suggested. "More of us would be able to go to the homeless shelter, attend events and visit other convents..."

"If we had enough money, yes." Mother Speranza nodded. "A minibus would be ideal. I'd like you to liaise with Alessia and organise our New Year's Eve celebrations."

"I will."

But when Sister Luce pitched her plan for the night to Alessia, the producer wasn't impressed.

"A three-hour prayer vigil? That's not going to entertain our viewers," she said.

"It'd be a service of thanksgiving with singing and prayers. The chapel looks lovely in candlelight," Sister Luce explained.

Alessia wasn't convinced. "We need a party."

Eventually they agreed to a short prayer service followed by more conventional New Year's Eve entertainments, starting with an evening meal, including the traditional New Year's Eve pig's trotters with lentils and polenta. Board games and karaoke would follow until midnight, when there would be a fireworks display in front of a bonfire.

Sister Luce had some objections about the karaoke, but was reassured that she wouldn't be made to sing on her own.

\*\*\*

On the night of New Year's Eve, the thanksgiving service was perfect. The songs were moving, the candlelight was cosy and everyone got the chance to contribute a prayer of thanks for the year that had just passed.

Sister Deodata gave thanks for the convent's new tractor, Sister Silvestra for the chestnut harvest, and Mother Speranza for the opportunity to be in a documentary. This made

Alessia grin with pleasure.

Sister Luce was grateful for so much that it would have taken her a whole day to list everything. And she was too shy to say anything aloud, so she gave her thanks in silence instead.

But as soon as the service was over, Alessia and Leonia pounced on her.

"What about you, Sister Luce? Are you thankful for anything?" Alessia asked her in front of Leonia's camera.

"I'm grateful for having no regrets for the past year," she said candidly. "Having no regrets or making peace with the ones you've got makes you happy and serene."

Everyone gathered in the recreation room and party hats, trumpets and blowers were handed out. They played bingo, followed by karaoke, then they moved to the garden where they lit a bonfire and had fun making shapes with sparklers for the camera.

At the stroke of midnight, the convent's bells pealed and the fireworks started.

"Thank you for organising this party," Mother Speranza told Alessia and Sister Luce.

"With tonight's filming we've finished the introduction to the convent. Next week we'll start the challenge," Alessia replied.

"Challenge?" Mother Speranza repeated.

"The question the documentary is going to answer: Is the convent still relevant to today's women? It's all in the contract."

"I wasn't aware…" Mother Speranza blanched.

She, Sister Luce and Sister Renata had pored over the contract but it was hard to understand, so they'd sent it to a solicitor and were reassured it was legal and reasonable.

"Next weekend four women will arrive to stay with you until May," Alessia explained.

Mother Speranza looked stunned and Sister Luce's heart went out to her. Did she regret signing the contract? Sister Luce imagined how unpleasant it must be to have such a regret.

"We can put them up in the pilgrims' guesthouse," she suggested.

"No. They'll have to stay in the convent with you," Alessia replied. "They've got to share your life. It'll be very exciting."

But Mother Speranza didn't look excited.

## 10. RETHINK THE SINK

Mother Speranza and all the nuns gathered in the convent's courtyard to welcome the four women who would be living with them for the next few months.

The producer introduced them. Dina was seventy-four and a retired headteacher. Matilde, who went by her *nom de guerre*, Hilda, was sixty-eight and had been a journalist and war correspondent. Giorgia, aged thirty-four, was a social worker. She had cycled to the convent and was vegan. Alba, a twenty-six-year-old office worker, would never part from her phone—so don't try, the producer warned them.

Mother Speranza welcomed them and told them that Sister Luce would be looking after them. "During your time with us you will join in our communal work, prayer and relaxation. Because, above all, we are a community."

"Yes to commune-living!" Hilda cried,

raising her fist.

"What if we just want to do our own things?" Alba asked, clutching her phone.

"There will be time for rest too," Mother Speranza said. "Sister Luce will give you a printed schedule of every day of the week."

"Do you mean we can't choose how to spend our time?" Alba asked.

"You can choose how to spend your free time."

Alba's eyebrows shot up.

"You'll be assigned a different job every week," Mother Speranza continued. "It might not be your favourite, but I ask you to bear with it."

Alba didn't look convinced. Mother Speranza explained that Sister Luce would accompany them to their rooms and they'd be expected downstairs again as soon as they had unpacked.

Alba's luggage looked like it might take a long time to unpack. Sister Luce helped carry one of the two large suitcases up the stairs, while Alba complained about the lack of a lift.

The other three had much less luggage, especially Giorgia, who had arrived by bike. She was very pleased with her room, especially because of the woodlands view.

Dina and Hilda were pleased with their

rooms too. They said they had expected windowless cells with a hard bed, a scratchy blanket and a chamber pot.

Sister Luce pointed out that a convent wasn't a prison, but admitted that the four guests had been given more comforts than the nuns would normally have, like mirrors, feather duvets and coffee makers.

Alba, however, wasn't at all pleased with her room. "How will I fit my stuff into this cupboard? You must have a bigger wardrobe."

"I have only two habits," Sister Luce replied candidly.

Alba gave Sister Luce a once over. "You're a pretty woman. You shouldn't be here."

"Where should I be?" Sister Luce asked, confused.

"Out there, partying, having fun!"

"But I like it here." Sister Luce thought of her hens, of praying and singing in the chapel, of sitting in the garden with her fellow sisters. "I have plenty of fun here, and you will too." She smiled and offered Alba her printed schedule for the week. "This week you'll be working in the kitchen."

"I don't work in the kitchen," Alba said, folding her arms. "My nails will get damaged."

"But this is what the Mother Superior has assigned you to do."

"Do you always do what she tells you?"

"Yes," Sister Luce said candidly. "I've taken a vow of obedience."

Alba's eyebrows shot up. "Well, I haven't, so I won't work in the kitchen. That's the place of women's servitude. I won't be chained to the sink."

Sister Luce didn't know what to do for a moment, but then she had an idea.

"Perhaps it's time for women to rethink the sink," she suggested. "We could claim the kitchen back, make it no longer a place of servitude but a space to express our creativity and share our love through food. Cooking for the convent, you wouldn't be serving a man," Sister Luce explained. "You'd be sharing love with the sisterhood."

Alba's eyes sparkled. "I like the idea. Hashtag reclaimthesink!"

## 11. STITCH THEM UP!

A week had passed since the guests' arrival at the convent and Sister Luce felt that the four women were settling in well. But today was the start of a new week, and that meant a changeover of duties.

Sister Luce was concerned about Alba but, when Mother Speranza told her that she'd be working in the chestnut grove, the glamorous young woman grinned and said that it would be great for selfies.

Sister Luce was relieved. She was assigned to chaperone the documentary crew in the sewing workshop, where Dina would work with Sisters Maddalena and Teodora.

The two nuns welcomed Dina warmly. As they showed her the embroidered altar cloths and priests' vestments they were working on, Dina's eyes sparkled. "That's *punto antico* embroidery! That's *tombolo* lace! My grandma used to do them," Dina reminisced.

"She wanted to teach me but I refused," she added with regret.

"We can teach you now," Sister Teodora offered.

Sister Luce quickly set up a station with a three-legged table, tubular tombolo pillow and several bobbins with thread. The two nuns showed Dina the ropes.

"This is just what Grandma used to do," Dina said, misty-eyed as she flicked the bobbins up and down around each other. "Grandma would be so proud of me now."

"Maybe she's looking down from heaven right now," Sister Maddalena replied.

Dina sighed. "I didn't let her teach me because she wanted to make linen for my wedding trousseau. I wouldn't hear of marriage and had no intention of spending my life darning my husband's socks. Now I realise that I should have taken her offer for what it really was: an expression of her love and her desire to keep the art alive."

"Well, what you're making now is certainly not for your trousseau," Sister Teodora reassured her. "This lace is going on a surplice—the tunic priests wear during liturgical services."

Dina froze. Her smile drained. "I'm not making clothes for a man," she declared, putting down the bobbins.

Sister Teodora and Sister Maddalena looked at each other in confusion, then at Sister Luce for guidance.

"Priests are men, but they don't lord it over women. At least, they shouldn't. They serve the community," Sister Luce said.

She thought of Father Anselmo who, well past retirement age, trundled up to the convent every day at the crack of dawn in his little car—come rain, snow or shine.

But Dina didn't budge. "I will not sew for a man! Stitch up the patriarchy!"

She got up and left the room.

Sister Luce gave Dina some time to cool off, then headed over to her room, bracing herself for the worst.

But when she knocked, a jolly voice replied from the inside. "Come in."

Dina was sitting at her desk in front of a laptop. She showed Sister Luce the laptop's screen.

"These are the people I'm going to make lace for," she announced, beaming.

It showed the website of a women's shelter.

"I used to volunteer there," Dina explained. "Every now and then, a baby was born. The mother received lots of useful gifts, but never anything like a christening gown."

"That's a great idea," Sister Luce agreed.

Sister Teodora and Sister Maddalena were extremely excited at the idea of working on a baby's gown. Dolls were sourced as mannequins, and Dina and Sister Maddalena worked on the lace while Sister Teodora sewed the gown. Sister Luce fetched items, kept the room tidy and did odd jobs.

At the end of the day, Sister Luce reported everything to Mother Speranza.

"Wouldn't it be nice if we could continue to make gowns for the shelter after Dina has left?" she asked the Mother Superior.

"I think that's a very good idea. I will contact the shelter."

When the gown was finished, it was shown to the rest of the community, and everyone agreed that it would make an exquisite baby shower present.

## 12. DRESSING DOWN

Mother Speranza assigned Sister Luce to the sewing workshop again.

"This week, Hilda will be with you. You'll have to work on the priests' vestments this time or we'll fall behind on orders," she warned her.

The good news was that Alessia and Leonia weren't going to be filming that week. But Sister Luce remembered Dina's reaction to sewing the priests' vestments, so she broached the matter with Hilda as gently as she could.

"I don't mind sewing clothes for men," Hilda replied good-naturedly. "It's a normal part of the division of labour. Back home I live in a commune too."

Sister Luce had never viewed the convent as a commune but she was relieved by Hilda's reaction. At least there would be no trouble this week.

Sisters Teodora and Maddalena welcomed

Hilda with enthusiasm and everyone got to work happily together.

After a while, Hilda wiped her forehead. "Don't you find this room too warm?"

"We need to keep it warm because we can't hold a needle properly with cold fingers," Sister Teodora explained.

"Could you wear a fleece or a jumper?" Hilda suggested helpfully.

"Our habits are a sign of our identity," Sister Maddalena explained.

"I see."

Hilda resumed working, fanning herself with a piece of cardboard, and none of them thought about the matter anymore.

Later, however, much to everyone's surprise, Hilda walked into the refectory wearing shorts and a strappy vest.

Mother Speranza approached Sister Luce. "Could you have a quiet word with Hilda about our dress code?"

Sister Luce agreed to the job and was about to do it when a thought came to her. What if Hilda was making a statement? Sister Luce didn't want to be dragged into an argument. Maybe, if they didn't give it attention, the problem would fizzle out on its own. Sister Luce decided not to say anything.

At evening prayers Hilda sauntered into the

chapel still dressed for the beach.

Mother Speranza darted a meaningful glance at Sister Luce, who resigned herself to the need to take action.

Thankfully she had an idea that might solve the problem without a confrontation.

When nobody was looking, Sister Luce sneaked down to the basement, where a boiler kept the convent deliciously toasty. Reluctantly, Sister Luce adjusted the thermostat's temperature. Hopefully Hilda would feel the change and put on more appropriate clothes.

As the convent's temperature dropped, the nuns walked around more briskly, rubbing their hands and blowing on them.

Unfortunately Hilda only changed into a sleeveless dress. It was progress, but not enough, so Sister Luce lowered the heating thermostat half a degree further. How much longer could she keep the rest of the convent shivering? Would Hilda capitulate before everyone else froze?

With this on her mind, Sister Luce went to the chapel to pray for a speedy resolution. She saw a magazine on Mother Speranza's pew—a brochure for thermal underwear. What a good idea!

Sister Luce rushed to the Mother Superior's

office, where she found Mother Speranza shivering at her desk.

"Could we order thermal undergarments for everyone? They would keep us warm under our habits. We would save on our heating bills and be more environmentally friendly," Sister Luce suggested.

The Mother Superior thought it was a great idea and twenty-two sets of thermal undergarments were ordered and gratefully received by every nun next day.

When they gathered in the chapel, Hilda turned up in woolly tights, a thick skirt and woolly jumper, and Sister Luce breathed a sigh of relief.

After prayers, Sister Luce heard Hilda chatting to Mother Speranza.

"I'm pleased you've given up on keeping the convent so hot. It will save your pocket and the environment. I'm glad you took the hint when I dressed lighter and left the thermal underwear brochure on your pew."

Mother Speranza looked confused, but thanked Hilda, and Sister Luce gave a secret smile.

## 13. CHAINS OF EVENTS

After the sewing workshop, Sister Luce was delighted when Mother Speranza assigned her to the chestnut grove with Giorgia.

Immediately after breakfast, the two women and the TV crew headed to the grove where Sister Silvestra was waiting.

The nun in charge of the grove had just started talking about pruning and grafting when one of the grove's workers ran up to them.

"Sisters, there's bad news!" Anita cried, panting. "The mayor has published plans to cut down the grove and build a hotel!"

"He can't do that on our land," Giorgia replied.

"Unfortunately this grove belongs to the town. It's only been entrusted to the convent's care," Sister Silvestra explained.

"And the hotel will be owned by the mayor's family," Anita explained.

"There's no hope then," Sister Silvestra conceded despondently.

"You can't give up!" Giorgia exclaimed. "You've vowed obedience to Mother Superior, not to him," Giorgia pointed out.

Her reasoning made sense and the three women went to Mother Speranza to report the news.

The Mother Superior listened carefully. "What do the residents think?"

"They don't want to lose the grove, but they also want the jobs that the hotel will bring," Sister Silvestra admitted.

"Why doesn't the mayor build his hotel on some other land?" Giorgia asked.

"All the land round here belongs to a duke who won't sell it or let anyone touch it," Mother Speranza explained.

"Then the mayor must have thought that he had better chances with you. Unless you make yourselves heard, he will always push you around. You must do something," Giorgia implored.

"I'll write to him," Mother Speranza said.

"Can we do something too?" Sister Luce asked.

"Do whatever you think might stop the chainsaws," Mother Speranza replied and dismissed them.

"We'll chain ourselves to the trees," Giorgia suggested.

"There are chains in the tractor barn, used for hauling felled trees," a delighted Sister Silvestra put in.

Sister Luce wasn't at all keen on being chained to anything, but Alessia and Leonia thought it would make for a great filming opportunity, so it was agreed.

They rallied in other sisters as volunteers. Giorgia helped them chain themselves to the trees, then finally chained herself.

Anita spread word in town, and it wasn't long before the local press scrambled up the mountain for the scoop.

"We won't leave until the mayor vows to leave the grove alone!" Giorgia declared to the journalists.

Sister Luce looked with apprehension at the ominous sky. Would the mayor capitulate before the impending storm?

Sister Silvestra was telling the journalists about the many uses of chestnuts and their flour, when the mayor turned up. All the journalists turned their attention to him.

"I will not let anyone build a hotel on this grove!" he declared as if he hadn't been the one to put forward the plan. "I will defend the chestnut grove, no matter the cost!"

Everyone whose hands weren't chained clapped. Giorgia unchained herself with the key she had in her pocket, then offered to help the sisters.

"I don't have my key," Sister Silvestra revealed.

Sister Luce didn't have hers either, and neither did any of the other nuns. They had left them in the barn. Meanwhile, the sky had turned black.

As the barn was quite a trek away, Giorgia asked the mayor to give her a lift to the barn, so off they went.

When they returned to the grove and unchained the nuns, the first drops of rain had started to fall. The mayor was roped in to give the nuns lifts back and forth to the convent.

When the mayor had delivered the last nun and was able to go home, the storm broke loose.

From her bedroom window, safe and dry, Sister Luce watched him drive under the torrential rain. She was sure he would not be scheming against the chestnut grove ever again.

## 14. THE BISHOP'S VISIT

"The bishop is visiting us tomorrow," Mother Speranza told Sister Luce.

The young nun wondered why the Mother Superior was sharing this information with her. She wasn't in charge of the liturgy, the catering or anything other than a small flock of hens.

"Alessia has asked to interview him for the documentary, but he declined," Mother Speranza continued. "I fear Alessia will persist. I wouldn't like him to be harassed. He's a shy man and he wouldn't like it."

Sister Luce knew about shyness and could fully empathise with him.

"I want him to enjoy his visit," Mother Superior went on, "also because I'll ask him to help us get a minibus for our convent. Can I ask you to keep a close watch so that nobody gives him any trouble?"

Sister Luce agreed.

On the day of the visit, she was in the

kitchen with Hilda—dressed smart—and Sister Veronica, the convent's cook. Alessia and Leonia had been filming them all morning as they prepared the lunch for the bishop's visit.

Sister Luce heard a car pull into the convent's car park. Next, Alessia and Leonia disappeared. It didn't take Sister Luce much to guess that the producer and the camerawoman must have gone in search of the bishop.

She ran out into the car park and found them behind a bush with their camera.

"Hi!" Sister Luce greeted them.

They jumped.

"Oh, hi! We were just filming some beautiful plants." Alessia gestured vaguely at a patch of stinging nettles.

"But you're supposed to be filming in the kitchen today," Sister Luce said.

"Nettles make excellent soup…" Leonia volunteered.

But Sister Luce wasn't fooled and was determined to stop them harassing the bishop as he got out of his car.

"Nettle soup, what a great idea! Let's pick some nettles."

Sister Luce showed them how to pick nettles without getting stung, and while the three of them collected the plants, the bishop got out of his car and entered the convent blissfully unaware.

They brought their pickings back to the kitchen and got to work making nettle soup, while Alessia and Leonia filmed.

They'd barely finished making the soup when Alessia and Leonia disappeared again. It was almost time for the Mass and Sister Luce had a terrible suspicion.

She ran to the chapel and found the pair outside the sacristy where the bishop was getting ready for the service.

"Caught you! I know what you're up to," Sister Luce challenged them.

Alessia and Leonia said that they were sorry and promised that they wouldn't try to ambush the bishop anymore.

Only after they had packed away their recording equipment into the car did Sister Luce let them into the chapel.

The bishop didn't notice anything and the service went on without glitches.

Straight after, it was time for lunch.

Everyone moved to the refectory and the bishop was seated between Mother Speranza and Sister Luce, with Hilda facing him on the other side of the table. Sister Luce could relax.

She'd just started on the delicious soup, when she overheard Hilda's conversation with the bishop.

"It would be a joint venture between us and the church to build new communes—or convents, if that's what you prefer to call them. We've secured funding and you can contribute several centuries' worth of expertise…"

Oh, no! Hilda was harassing the bishop with a business pitch! That must be why she had dressed up that morning.

But the bishop didn't look displeased.

"I'm not the person to speak to," he told Hilda with a good-natured smile. "You should speak to the real boss."

"But I don't believe in God," Hilda replied.

"I don't mean Him." He chuckled. "I mean the Mother General, who is in charge of all the nuns of this order all over the world. She's the real boss. This morning, Mother Speranza and I called her and she agreed to help Mother Speranza get a minibus."

Hilda looked pleased to hear that the boss was a woman, and the conversation moved on to the health benefits of nettle soup.

Now Sister Luce could finally relax.

## 15. THE BEST VALENTINE'S DAY

Before entering the convent, Sister Luce had had a fiancée. Every Valentine's Day he'd given her chocolates and flowers and taken her out for a meal.

Sister Luce didn't regret giving up the love of a man, but sometimes she wished she could still receive flowers and chocolates and be made a fuss of on Valentine's Day. Instead, every Valentine's, a delegation from the convent would take gifts to the homeless shelter in town.

This year, Mother Speranza asked her to take their four guests and the TV crew.

"I object to taking gifts. It's a consumeristic habit," Hilda complained.

"I'm okay with gifts if they're environmentally friendly," Giorgia put in.

"And useful," Dina added. "The last thing a homeless person needs is clutter."

They brainstormed possibilities, but every useful gift they could think of had already been given at Christmas.

"How about we treat them to a show? We could do songs and dances that everyone can join in with," Hilda suggested.

Everyone liked the idea, especially Alba, who planned to stream it on her social media account, and Alessia, who felt it would look great in the documentary.

Only Sister Luce wasn't so keen. She hated the prospect of performing in public. But they needed her to make up numbers for the dances, so she relented.

They chose a repertoire of traditional songs from all regions of Italy, and tarantella songs that easily could be danced to alone, in groups or in pairs.

They rehearsed with gusto in the convent's recreation room, and even Sister Luce enjoyed the dancing.

On Valentine's Day they filled Dina and Alba's car with guitars, shakers and tambourines, and set off for the town.

At the shelter, the show had been eagerly awaited. Tables and chairs were pushed to the sides to make space for dancing and a makeshift stage had been erected just for the show.

At the sight of the stage, Sister Luce's courage drained. Before she could get over the shock, she was ushered up the steps to find herself standing on the stage in front of the hall with Leonia's camera pointed at her.

It took all Sister Luce's courage for her to remain there instead of running away, and she had none left to sing or dance.

So when Alba threaded her arm through Sister Luce's to start turning with the tarantella, Sister Luce remained frozen. Alba launched herself into the spin, but Sister Luce didn't follow. Alba was yanked back like a ball at the end of a rope and recoiled into Sister Luce. They reeled, staggered and would have fallen if Hilda hadn't caught them.

Everyone clapped, assuming the unusual dance step had been part of the act.

But Sister Luce was mortified. Determined not to cause any more near-misses, she pushed any thoughts other than the steps out of her mind, and proceeded with the dance routine.

After what felt like an eternity, the show was over and a roaring applause told the performers their efforts were appreciated.

Sister Luce still felt mortified and longed to return to the safety of her convent and to hide behind her veil in the back of the chapel. This must be her worst Valentine's Day ever.

She was helping pack up the instruments, feeling sorry for herself, when Giacoma, who was in charge of the shelter, came up to her.

"Thank you so much! Today has been the shelter's best Valentine's Day ever!" she declared. "We'd like to thank you with a little Valentine's gift of our own too."

She asked Sister Luce to follow her back onto the stage. Reluctantly, Sister Luce climbed the steps, with Leonia's camera still filming.

"On behalf of all the volunteers and guests, a little present from the bottom of our hearts," Giacoma said.

Someone handed Sister Luce a bunch of pink roses and a large box with a see-through lid. It contained twenty-six heart-shaped chocolates, each carved with the names of the convents' nuns and the four guests.

Tears pricked Sister Luce's eyes. She was going to cry on stage—and in front of Leonie's camera—but she didn't care. This was her best Valentine's ever.

## 16. TESTING TIMES

Sister Luce looked at the four women who had agreed to try out the life of her convent for four months. They had come a long way since those difficult first few days, and they looked happy and settled now, Sister Luce thought as they worked together in the pilgrims' guesthouse. Some dusted and vacuumed the rooms, others cleaned the toilets. Sister Luce and Alba were making beds.

"Sister, I can't take this," Alba said suddenly.

"I'll help you," Sister Luce said, coming over and taking a corner of the heavy mattress.

"No, Sister. I didn't mean the mattress. It's the whole being here that I can't take any more. Always working and praying, wearing the same few clothes I brought with me…"

Sister Luce remembered the enormous suitcase Alba had struggled to drag up the stairs and wondered how that amount of clothes could be insufficient, but she didn't say it.

"... I haven't been to my hairdresser for weeks and my regrowth is showing," Alba rattled on.

Sister Luce thought that her veil was great for that.

"...and I miss home, my family and my friends."

On this last point, Sister Luce could fully empathise. She too had missed her family and friends when she joined the convent, and sometimes still did.

"You can leave anytime. Have you talked to Mother Speranza and Alessia?"

"No. But you're right, I should," Alba replied, and continued making the bed.

Later that day, Sister Luce asked the producer if Alba had talked to her.

"Yes, she has," Alessia replied. "I told her that she can leave the documentary anytime, but she will only get paid for the days she's been here. So she's decided to stay."

This wasn't the answer Sister Luce had hoped for. If Alba was staying just for the money, she'd surely continue to be unhappy.

The next morning, Alba didn't turn up for morning prayer in the chapel. Instead, she traipsed into the refectory late for breakfast and looking dishevelled.

"This coffee is undrinkable! This bread is stale—only good for the pigs!" she complained aloud.

Mother Speranza arched her eyebrows but didn't say a word. Sister Luce guessed why Alba was in such a foul mood but she couldn't think what to do to make things better for her.

Afterwards, when it was time to work at the pilgrims' guesthouse, Alba folded her arms and refused to go.

Today, Alessia and Leonia had planned to film Alba and Sister Luce at work as chambermaids but, faced with Alba's stubborn refusal, they went off to film someone else and Alba spent the morning shut in her room.

Sister Luce reported to Mother Speranza what had happened.

"I feel sorry for her. She misses home and would like to leave but she's staying on because of the money. Is there anything we can do to make her stay with us a little happier?" Sister Luce asked.

"Yes. We could let her choose which chores she'd like to do. But we need to do it discreetly, so the others don't feel that we have favourites."

Sister Luce went to see Alba in her room and announced that Mother Speranza allowed her to choose her chores.

Alba looked a little surprised. "There's nothing I want to do," she said.

Sister Luce made suggestions but Alba shot down every one. By now, it was lunchtime. In the refectory, again, Alba complained loudly about the food, sending glances at Mother Speranza, but the Mother Superior didn't react.

During the afternoon, Alba refused to join in the games at recreation time, and she disappeared when it was time to work. That evening in the chapel, she didn't turn her phone off and, when it rang loudly in the middle of the service, she took the call and carried on a loud conversation on her dislike for the convent. Everyone heard every word, including Mother Speranza. The Mother Superior just paused the prayer and waited patiently for Alba to end the call. Then, she prayed for "all those who aren't happy in their current job or situation."

Alba looked taken aback by Mother Speranza's kind gesture and forgiveness.

Sister Luce, too, was surprised, but by something else. Sitting next to Alba, she had seen that her phone hadn't rung with a call but with an alarm. Alba must have set it up in advance, and her "conversation" was nothing more than her talking to herself.

Sister Luce didn't know what to think. As

soon as they left the chapel, she confronted Alba. The young woman burst into tears.

"Alessia told me that I wouldn't get the rest of the money if I left the documentary now, but I need that money. So I decided to get myself expelled from the convent. I behaved badly on purpose so that Mother Speranza would kick me out. Instead, she's been so patient, kind and forgiving... Thank you, Sister, for putting up with me! I've never felt so loved. And now I feel very guilty for treating you like that!"

"It's okay," Sister Luce reassured her, squeezing her hand.

"I don't feel homesick anymore and I want to stay here till the end," Alba said, throwing her arms around Sister's shoulders.

"That's great," Sister Luce said with a big smile.

## 17. BIRTHDAY TWINS

Being an only child and grandchild, Sister Luce had never had to share her parents' and grandparents' love with any siblings or cousins. As the best student at her school, she'd also had a considerable share of her teachers' love.

Until entering the convent, the only love Sister Luce had had to share was God's love—with eight billion people, no less. But that was fine because God was capable of doing the impossible.

Mother Speranza, on the other hand, was only a human, and Sister Luce found sharing her love with the rest of the convent's sisters a little trickier.

Today it was Sister Luce's birthday, and the one day in the year when she could expect to be the recipient of the Mother Superior's undivided attention.

Whenever it was someone's birthday, Mother Speranza would announce it at breakfast and, for the rest of the day, every prayer would include a special mention for her.

The birthday sister also had the privilege to choose the cake that would be baked by the convent's cook, Sister Veronica, and served at dinner with candles for blowing.

That morning at breakfast, Sister Luce waited expectantly for Mother Speranza to make the announcement.

"Today we pray especially for Sister Luce, who's turning twenty-five today," the Mother Superior said, but then continued, "and for Sister Grazia, who is turning twenty-six."

Sister Luce was stunned. That day had always been her special day, but now Sister Grazia had arrived they would always have to share it!

Sister Luce felt guilty about her feelings. After all, it wasn't Sister Grazia's fault. Maybe she felt equally upset to have her special day encroached upon.

But Sister Grazia didn't seem to mind at all. Quite the opposite, actually.

All through that day, Sister Grazia kept smiling at Sister Luce and, whenever their paths crossed, Sister Grazia greeted her with, "Hello, twin!"

It made Sister Luce feel even guiltier.

At one point, when Sister Luce was tending

to her hens, Sister Veronica bounded down the field towards her.

She must be coming to ask her to choose the cake, Sister Luce thought.

"I guess you know why I've come here," Sister Veronica told her with a big smile.

"You want me to choose my cake," Sister Luce answered with delight.

Sister Veronica's face fell. "Actually, because Sister Grazia has just arrived, Mother Speranza thought it would be nice to let her choose the cake. You don't mind, do you?"

Sister Luce tried not to show her disappointment. "Of course not," she replied cheerfully,

Sister Veronica then asked Sister Luce for some eggs for the cake—which was the reason she had come to see her—and left.

For the rest of the day Sister Luce felt sad, and then guilty for feeling sad.

When the cake appeared at dinnertime, it was a pistachio cake, her least favourite, and it had only one candle. She and Sister Grazia would have to share even the candle!

"I didn't know whether to put twenty-five candles or twenty-six," Sister Veronica explained, "so I decided to go with one."

"That's nice," Sister Grazia said, "because one is the difference between our ages. If we blow it away, we become twins."

It was a sweet idea, Sister Luce thought.

As everyone started singing *Tanti Auguri a Te*, Sister Luce and Sister Grazia blew out the candle together and Sister Luce made a wish: that her jealousy could be extinguished with the candle's fire.

The cake wasn't pistachio after all, but pandan, a south-east Asian flavour that Sister Grazia had encountered when she was training in their convent in Singapore—and it was delicious.

After the meal, Sister Grazia approached Sister Luce.

"When I was growing up, back home in the Philippines, I was sad because I had no brothers or sisters. Now I have so many sisters and even a birthday twin. Thank you for making this my best birthday ever."

Sister Luce felt her heart swell with love and gratitude. What did it matter if she'd had to share all the birthday perks and attentions when she had gained the love of a twin?

## 18. THE CARNIVAL PARADE

"Shall we take part?" Hilda asked Sister Luce, passing her the local newspaper with an article about the upcoming carnival parade.

"We're more about Lent than carnival here," Sister Luce replied with a smile, glancing at the paper with a photo of people wearing beautiful Venetian masks.

Sister Luce had never liked masks and found them unsettling. What was the point of hiding one's true self? And those were only the physical masks. The emotional ones were even more unhelpful, she felt.

That afternoon, at recreation time, Mother Speranza made an announcement:

"The volunteers at the homeless shelter are joining the parade with their own float to raise money to refurbish their premises. They've asked us to help, going through the crowd with donation buckets. I've agreed."

Alessia and Leonia were delighted to include

such an event in the documentary.

An excited Hilda planned to dress up as Che Guevara, Dina as a suffragette and Giorgia as Mother Earth. But Alba had other ideas.

The next morning, four costumes, complete with masks and feathery headdresses, were delivered to the convent.

"I've rented one for each of us. They'll look great on social media," Alba explained.

"I'm not wearing a gown," Giorgia announced. "I haven't worn a skirt since primary school. It's just not me."

"But that's the point of masquerading: being someone else," Dina pointed out.

Hilda said that the costume was already rented and, as none of the nuns would be wearing one, it'd be a waste if she didn't.

Giorgia hated waste even more than ballgowns, so she agreed.

The homeless shelter's float was a beautiful house with *All Welcome* painted over the wide-open front door. The four ladies were hoisted onto the float in a cloud of lace, tulle and feathers.

Sister Luce and the other nuns stayed on the ground with their donation tins and buckets. As the float set off and the nuns followed, bystanders commented that the nun costume must be the most popular this year as there were so many people dressed up as nuns.

A donor approached Sister Luce with a fifty euro note.

"Have you got change?" the man asked.

Sister Luce had taken a purse of change along, but had entrusted it to Giorgia, who had a pocket. And Giorgia was on the float.

"Yes. Please, bear with me," she replied to the man, and turned to the float to catch Giorgia's eye.

But which one of the four Venetian ladies was Giorgia? Sister Luce hadn't memorised her costume. She'd have to ask each of them for the purse. This required climbing on the float.

Unfortunately the float had four tiers and the Venetian ladies were at the top. With a steadying hand from Prince Charming and a leg up from the Big Bad Wolf, Sister clambered up while the crowd clapped in encouragement.

The first Venetian lady turned out to be Alba so, squeezing around Alba's gown, Sister Luce reached the next one. Unfortunately this was Hilda. Sister Luce was now on the most prominent spot of the float, in front of the house's door.

The next lady was Dina. Giorgia was the last and furthest of the four. She extracted the purse from a pocket she had sewn inside her petticoat and Sister Luce set off back down again.

The descent was as embarrassing as the ascent. When she finally landed on firm ground, the donor told her that she could keep the change after all, because he felt she had earned it.

"You could have shouted and I would have thrown the purse down," Giorgia told Sister Luce at the end of the parade.

"I didn't know which of the ladies you were. Up there, you behaved as ladylike as everyone else."

"I enjoyed playing the part of a lady," Giorgia admitted, "even if I didn't think I would. I always thought I was a tomboy, but maybe that was what other people thought of me and it became my mask."

"Are you saying that it's taken a carnival mask to set you free from your real one?" Sister Luce asked, and both women chuckled.

## 19. FASTING

Sister Luce had no trouble with the hardships of convent life. She could wake up early, go to bed late and do night vigils in the chapel. She could do hard physical work without complaint, and could stand the cold and the heat, wearing the same sandals and habit all year round.

But she struggled with one thing: fasting. Whenever she was hungry, she became cranky and unfit for anything.

Now the time of year she dreaded had arrived: Lent.

The forty days of prayer, almsgiving and fasting leading up to Easter began with Ash Wednesday, when the sisters would eat only one full meal.

Sister Luce couldn't believe it when Giorgia, Alba, Dina and Hilda announced that they'd join in the fasting too, despite Dina and Hilda being over the age limit the Church required.

On Ash Wednesday, Sister Luce kept to herself and worked at the henhouse, so she could be cranky only with herself and with her hens.

But Friday was another fasting day for them, and Sister Luce woke up crotchety in anticipation of what was to come.

On her way to morning prayers, she saw Mother Speranza walk towards her.

"Sister Luce, I need your help. Last night there was a theft from the pantry," Mother Speranza told her. "They stole vanilla pods and saffron. I don't want there to be another theft tonight. Could you please keep watch in the kitchen tonight?"

Sister Luce agreed. She never needed much sleep.

But that night, when she stepped into the kitchen, she regretted accepting the task. The pantry, the fridge, the shelves—everywhere was stacked with food, easily within her reach, and with no one looking. After a day of fasting, this was torture. The temptation was strong.

Did the night still count as fasting time? Technically the next day would start at midnight, so the fasting should be over.

It was enough of a reason to stay wide awake, waiting for the stroke of midnight like a hungry Cinderella who prefers a pumpkin to a carriage.

Sister Luce strategically positioned a chair in view of all doors and windows, made herself comfortable on it and started praying the rosary to while away the time.

She had no idea how she fell asleep, but when she woke up it was already morning and Sister Veronica stood in front of her with a compassionate smile.

"I gather you didn't catch any thieves. You must have been very tired!"

Sister Luce was mortified at her failure, and was even hungrier than before. It wasn't time for breakfast yet and she didn't feel like she could ask Sister Veronica for food—especially not after her blunder!

"There are six pots of jam and bread for breakfast..." Sister Veronica rattled on, taking stock to rule out any theft.

Sister Luce's mouth watered and her stomach rumbled. Thankfully no thefts had taken place that night. Sister Luce felt a little less guilty, but just as hungry.

She and Sister Veronica joined the others in the chapel. There the silences were filled by the loud rumbles of Sister Luce's stomach.

At the end of morning prayers, it took Sister Luce all she had not to run to the refectory like a child on Christmas morning.

There a surprise welcomed them.

A glittery banner hung on the wall: *Happy International Women's Day*.

The table was decorated with yellow mimosa blossoms, and a beautiful vanilla and saffron cake sat on the counter.

Hilda, Dina, Alba and Giorgia stood together smiling, watching the surprise on the faces of the others.

"We thought we'd celebrate Women's Day, even if it's Lent," Hilda explained.

"Especially here, where everyone is a woman," Dina added.

"Where did you buy such a beautiful cake?" Sister Veronica asked.

"We baked it in Sister Silvestra's workshop. We had to take ingredients from your pantry," Alba admitted.

"So you were the culprits!" Mother Speranza exclaimed with relief.

Sister Luce got two generous portions of cake for her troubles, and her stomach was finally full.

## 20. AGONY AUNT

The afternoon's relaxation hour was truly relaxing for Sister Luce only when they weren't being filmed. But today this wasn't the case.

"Sit with us, Sister," Alba called from the corner where the four guests of the convent sat.

Sister Luce joined them with her crochet.

"We're sharing our heartbreak stories," Alba recapped for her. "What's yours?"

"I don't have one," Sister Luce replied.

"You must have a heartbreak story or you wouldn't be here," Dina declared.

"Isn't heartbreak the reason women abandon the world and take the veil?" Hilda asked.

"Not at all!" Sister Luce cried. "I had a fiancé and we were very happy together."

Only after she'd made the revelation did Sister Luce notice she was being filmed.

"Then why did you enter the convent?"

Giorgia asked with interest.

"Tell us your story," the documentary's producer said, and the others echoed her.

Sister Luce's simple comment was turning into an interview.

Since the beginning of the documentary, she had managed to blend into the background. An interview would put her at the centre of attention, which she hated.

"You can't refuse us, because a nun's job is to tell others about God and how he touched her life," Alba reminded her.

Sister Luce couldn't disagree with that, especially as her call had started with meeting a nun who had inspired her with her joy and her words. How could she refuse to do the same for others who would watch the documentary?

So Sister Luce told them about that inspirational meeting, how she tried to ignore her growing desire to enter the convent but it wouldn't go away.

She explained to them how, every time she imagined herself married, she didn't feel the same joy as when she imagined herself in a convent. From the moment she made her decision, that joy never left her, even through the difficult time of saying bye to friends and family and to her fiancé.

Telling him that he was no longer part of her

life's plan had been the hardest part. Thankfully he'd eventually fallen in love with someone else and they'd married.

"How do you feel about that?" Giorgia asked.

"I'm very happy for him."

The following day, Alba approached Sister Luce.

"I've told my social media followers about your interview and they've sent me lots of questions. Can you help me answer them?"

"What sort of questions?" Sister Luce asked.

Alba offered her a phone and Sister Luce read aloud.

*I want to break up with my boyfriend, but I don't want to hurt him. How can I do it painlessly*, one girl asked.

*How do I decide if this relationship is right for me*, another one asked.

Sister Luce gave her advice, Alba relayed it to her followers and Sister Luce felt that she had accomplished her duty.

The next day more requests arrived. Sister Luce answered those too, and more on the following day. She'd become an agony aunt and she enjoyed it!

She felt she was helping other people and, perhaps, bringing them closer to God.

But as time passed and the flow of questions

didn't stop, Sister Luce started wondering if what she was doing was right. She didn't want to become a social media celebrity.

Mother Speranza had agreed to the documentary, but not to one of her nuns becoming a social media influencer.

Sister Luce told the Mother Superior what was happening and asked for her instructions and advice.

"Social media fame is uncharted territory for us," Mother Speranza said pensively. "Perhaps it would be a good idea to step back from it until we've decided what to do."

Sister Luce didn't need to be told twice. She rushed to tell Alba that she was to step out of the social media limelight.

"Don't worry, Sister Luce. You don't have to step back at all," Alba said with a smile. "I have watched and listened to you give your careful answers. I will carry on replying to the questions in a similar way."

"Amen to that." Sister Luce smiled.

## 21. PIGSTY

It was the start of another week and time to redistribute the weekly chores amongst the convent's four guests. Sister Luce didn't like that task because it inevitably upset someone and she hated upsetting people.

"Please don't give me the pigsty. I can't bear the smell of pigs," Dina pleaded.

Sister Luce's sheet of chores from Mother Speranza did have Dina down for the pigsty, but before Sister Luce could break the news, the convent's doorbell rang.

Sister Luce went to the door to find an older gentleman asking for Dina.

"Is she expecting you?"

"No," the man replied, shifting uncomfortably on his feet. "You can tell her it's her brother, Riccardo."

Sister Luce returned to the others.

"Your brother, Riccardo, is here for you," she told Dina.

Her face turned the colour of the chapel's candles.

"Tell him that I'm not here," she said coldly.

"I can't lie."

"Then tell him that I don't want to see him. I will never forgive him for taking our parents' inheritance."

"If he's come all the way here to find you, maybe he wants to make amends," Sister Luce pointed out.

"You don't have any siblings, Sister Luce, so you can't understand," Dina snapped, then stormed out of the room.

Sister Luce was hurt by Dina's barbs, but this was often the way. Hurt people often hurt others until someone made an effort to stop the spread of hurt. And Sister Luce was determined to do just that.

She returned to the door where the man was waiting, looking hopeful.

"I'm sorry, Dina is not willing to see you," she told him.

"Please tell her I've come to apologise," he pleaded. "I have wanted to do it for years, but I couldn't find her because she moved. It was only when I saw your documentary's trailer on TV that I finally knew where to find her."

"I trust that, with time and perseverance, she might come round to it," Sister Luce continued.

"I will make all the time that's needed!" he replied eagerly.

Sister Luce spoke to Mother Speranza and they came up with a plan. Riccardo would stay at the pilgrims' guesthouse for a while to give Dina a chance to change her mind. Meanwhile, he would do chores around the convent. Hopefully Dina would see that he was serious about their reconciliation.

"For his chores, how about mucking out the pigsty?" Sister Luce suggested.

"It sounds like a humbling job for him to show his regret," Mother Speranza agreed.

Crucially, Sister Luce thought, it would spare Dina from having to do it.

Dina and Sister Luce were assigned to work in the vegetable patch. There was plenty of spring sowing to do, as well as an unimpeded view of the pigsty.

Later that morning, Dina and Sister Luce were planting peas when Dina's gaze fell on the pigsty and she froze.

"Who's that man mucking out the pigs?" she asked suspiciously.

"Your brother. He's staying with us, so we've put him to work. The pigsty had been assigned to you this week, but Mother Speranza asked him to do it in your place."

Dina didn't reply and she was very quiet for the rest of that day.

The next day, when they entered the chapel for morning prayer, Riccardo was there, kneeling on the furthest back pew.

"He's still here!" Dina whispered to Sister Luce.

During the bidding prayers, Mother Speranza prayed aloud for forgiveness and reconciliation wherever they were needed, and Sister Luce silently did the same.

When she got to the vegetable patch for another day's work, she spotted Dina and Riccardo talking over the pigsty's fence. She prayed that this conversation went well.

A little later, Dina joined her.

"Sister Luce, I'm not going to be at the refectory at lunchtime. Riccardo and I are going out for lunch to discuss sharing the family's estate. It's a lot of land and we're thinking of farming it together," Dina said with a shy smile.

"That's wonderful!" Sister Luce smiled.

Indeed, the Lord worked in mysterious ways.

## 22. NUN OF THE YEAR

Sister Luce felt good about herself. In the last few weeks she had conquered her shyness. She had given romantic advice to Alba's social media followers and reunited Dina with her brother. After all this good work she could certainly count herself as a good nun.

She was absorbed in these thoughts as she met Giorgia, Hilda, Alba and Dina.

"Here comes Sister Luce!" Dina cried.

"The Pope should be coming to give you a prize," Hilda said.

Sister Luce froze. "The Pope? A prize for me?"

"Oh, yes. He's coming to give you the Nun Of The Year award."

"But I wasn't told anything about it."

"It's a surprise," Giorgia replied.

"They want to catch your first reaction on camera," Alba said. "But we thought we should give you a heads-up so that you can get yourself ready—iron your veil, or whatever nuns do."

Sister Luce thanked them and rushed to the chapel, where she thanked God for the honour. There must be other nuns who had done bigger things than she had.

But maybe the documentary had given her more exposure. If this was happening even before the documentary was aired, what accolades might be bestowed on her after? The thought was dizzying.

She rushed downstairs, determined to be found hard at work by the Pope. But she was intercepted by Sister Veronica.

"I've run out of flour and we have a visitor for lunch," the cook nun said.

The visitor had to be the Pope, Sister Luce thought with a frisson of excitement.

"Could you go to town and buy some flour for me?" Sister Veronica continued.

Sister Luce would have said yes, but she couldn't be out of the convent when the Pope came! Clearly Sister Veronica didn't know the purpose of the Pope's visit.

"I'm sorry, but I can't leave the convent today," Sister Luce said mysteriously.

"Then could you look after the kitchen while I go?"

"Yes."

Sister Luce immediately regretted it. As she

deep-fried sardines and stirred pots, her habit was impregnated with fishy smells and her sleeves were splattered with tomato sauce.

Sister Veronica couldn't have come back too soon!

Sister Luce rushed back to her room to change into her spare habit, only to realise that it hadn't yet come back from the laundry!

Who could lend her a habit the right size? Her birthday twin, Sister Grazia!

"Normally I wouldn't mind the stains on my sleeves, but we're having a very important visitor today," Sister Luce whispered.

"Who is that?" Sister Grazia asked.

"I'm not allowed to say."

"How exciting!"

Unfortunately Sister Grazia's spare habit hadn't returned from the laundry either.

By now it was almost lunchtime and Sister Luce decided it was best to give up her quest for a clean habit, especially as she didn't want to tell more people about the visit.

But Sister Grazia had already spread the news and the whole convent was abuzz with excitement and speculations.

When they finally entered the refectory, all but the most health-conscious were sorely disappointed: their lunch guest was their GP, who had come for their checkup.

"You played an April Fools' prank on us all," Sister Grazia said good-naturedly.

Sister Luce bit her tongue and kept waiting for the Pope's arrival. He must be coming after lunch.

When the Pope still hadn't come at suppertime, she approached Giorgia and the others.

"Are you sure the Pope is coming today?"

Giorgia's eyes widened. "You still believe that? We thought you had worked it out by now, with today being the first of April..."

"So it was a prank?" Sister Luce asked.

"It started off as a misunderstanding," Hilda explained. "We said that you're such a good nun that the Pope should give you a prize, but you thought it was actually happening. As today is April Fools' Day, we couldn't resist playing along with it."

"We're sorry. Are you mad at us?" Alba asked gingerly.

Sister Luce chuckled. This was her just desert for thinking so much of herself that she had believed such a ridiculous idea.

"I'm not mad at all," she told them with a smile. "I'm flattered that you think I deserve a prize."

## 23. THE AVERAGE NUN

"I'm sorry to say that we'll be filmed this evening too," Sister Luce announced to the group of four women.

"That's fine, Sister Luce. We don't mind," Dina replied. "We volunteered to take part in this documentary. Didn't you?"

"No, I was asked. I still can't work out why Mother Speranza chose me," Sister Luce admitted.

"It's obvious why. You're not the average nun," Alba said, and the others nodded.

For the rest of that day, Sister Luce kept thinking about Alba's words. In what way wasn't she "the average nun"?

After her Nun Of The Year blunder, she wasn't going to imagine that she was above average. It was clear that, if she wanted to blend in and live a quiet life, she must become an average nun.

That evening in the chapel, Sister Luce sat

between Sister Benedetta and Sister Grazia. Both sang proficiently and loudly. Maybe this was what was required of the average nun.

Sister Luce amped up her volume and concentrated on the melody rather than the words. The improvement was so dramatic that it was picked up on by Leonia and the camerawoman zoomed in on Sister Luce.

This was the opposite of what she wanted! Sister Luce stopped and decided that singing would not be the field in which she would better herself.

The next day, in the sacristy, Sister Luce saw Sister Angelica folding altar linen neatly into a tidy drawer and concluded that the average nun was tidy.

She spent the best part of the morning tidying her shelves in the barn, arranging her hens' feed, oyster shells and anti-lice powder into alphabetical order. When she had completed the job, she looked at her shelves with satisfaction.

But later, when she returned to feed her hens, she forgot about the arrangement. She grabbed the anti-lice powder instead of the poultry feed, and the disinfectant instead of the tonic, and filled the feeding stations.

It was only when the birds refused to eat and drink that she realised her mistake and rushed to clean the trays.

She concluded that tidiness wasn't for her and she must find other ways to become an average nun.

Back in the main building, she met Sister Renata carrying a pile of magazines. Sister Luce didn't usually read them but, judging by the size of the pile, her fellow sisters did. The average nun must be a good reader.

Sister Luce took a bunch of magazines, and after lunch she went to her room and began to read. But she was so tired from the morning's extra work in the barn that she fell asleep at once.

She woke up to the sound of knocking at her door.

It was Mother Speranza.

"Are you all right?" the Mother Superior asked. "You didn't turn up for afternoon prayers."

Sister Luce was mortified to admit that she had fallen asleep. For the rest of the afternoon, she wondered what was so wrong with her that all her attempts at being a normal nun were failing miserably.

When she returned to her room for the night, she found the magazines still on her bed. An article caught her attention. The writer had interviewed several nuns. Some were missionary sisters, others had never left their convent, others wrote books and others worked in nursing homes.

That was it! There was no such a thing as an average nun. Even if they wore the same habit, each nun was as individual and unique as any other person.

Then what had Alba meant? There was only one way to find out.

"I meant that you are photogenic," Alba explained. "That's got to be why Mother Speranza chose you for the documentary."

Sister Luce chuckled. So that was it! It wasn't a moral attribute or a specific behaviour. It was just her appearance!

"And there I was, trying to become more average so that I wouldn't stand out anymore!" she admitted.

"You will always stand out." Dina smiled. "Nuns are not made to be invisible. Your life choices and vows—they're certainly not in the average person's lifestyle!"

Sister Luce thought that was right. With a little help from above, she would conquer her shyness and learn to cope with whatever attention life would throw at her.

## 24. IN DEBT

Sister Luce was looking forward to a quiet day plaiting palm fronds for the Palm Sunday procession. But when she went to Sister Silvestra to collect the palms, an unpleasant surprise awaited her.

"Someone left the greenhouse's windows open and last night's frost has ruined all our palms!" Sister Silvestra cried.

Sister Luce remembered showing the greenhouse to the TV crew and opening the windows. She must have forgotten to close them again!

"I'm very sorry. I'm the one who left the windows open," she confessed, mortified.

"Oh, well, it's a pity, but everyone makes mistakes. We'll have to use olive branches at the procession instead."

But Sister Luce couldn't forgive herself. She wished to be reproached so that the scores would be settled. Instead, through her forgiveness, Sister Silvestra had put her into debt to herself and the convent.

"In debt" was a place Sister Luce hated almost as much as "in sin". She would not have peace until she had procured palm fronds for the procession.

Without any money to buy some, all she could do was scout the land for any palms growing wild or in someone else's garden.

She found beech, hazel, chestnut and conifers on the convent's land, but no palms of any kind.

Eventually she spotted some in a private garden. She nervously walked to the gate and rang the intercom. Music wafted from inside. There must be a party.

Nobody answered the intercom. Perhaps they couldn't hear her over the music. She had better just help herself to the fronds overhanging the road, she thought, keen to avoid talking to strangers.

She cut the fronds with her penknife, letting them drop to the ground on her side of the wall.

But as she stretched her arm to reach a frond that was a little further, she dropped her penknife inside the garden. It was Sister Silvestra's knife—she couldn't leave it there!

Sister Luce hitched her skirt and climbed

over the wall and down the other side.

Having recovered the penknife and cut the frond, she attempted to climb back, but that turned out to be harder than the other way round.

However much she tried, she couldn't get a good footing. She was trapped inside a stranger's garden! Her only hope was to find a button to open the gate from the inside.

"Hey, where are you going?" someone called from behind her.

Sister Luce dropped the penknife and the frond and raised her hands in surrender. She was a thief and a trespasser!

In her attempt to pay back her debt with Sister Silvestra and the convent she had got herself into a bigger debt with the law! She should have conquered her shyness and rung the doorbell again instead of climbing over the wall.

Sister Luce turned towards the voice and froze. The person who had stopped her was a sheriff. He was going to handcuff her and take her to jail, she thought in a panic.

The man smiled and Sister Luce's panic subsided just enough for her to realise that something was odd. There were no sheriffs in Italy.

"The party's that way," the man said, "but if

you want to leave, the button to open the gate is there. I like your costume. It's very realistic."

So this was a fancy dress party and she had been mistaken for one of the guests! She wasn't going to be arrested after all!

She thanked the man, picked up her penknife and the frond from the ground and scuttled out through the gate.

She returned to the convent, her heart brimming with gratitude for her escape.

As she walked into the chapel late for the communal prayer time and nobody reproached her, she felt even more in debt than before: to the "sheriff" who showed her the way out, to the owner of the garden from which she had taken the palms, and to her Mother Superior and fellow sisters, who generously put up with her mistakes and lateness.

But from now on, Sister Luce wouldn't let being "in debt" bother her anymore.

## 25. AN UNEXPECTED BONUS

Knowing that their convent was hosting some visitors, the bishop invited everyone to attend Easter Mass at the cathedral.

Mother Speranza accepted gladly and the bishop kindly sent a minibus to collect everyone.

The ceremony was beautiful and, when it was over, Mother Speranza, Sister Luce and a small delegation thanked the bishop.

When they gave him their Easter wishes and a Colomba Easter cake—a type of dove-shaped panettone—the bishop smiled.

"I too have an Easter gift for you, but you'll have to find it first. In fact, I've prepared a little treasure hunt for you."

The nuns and visitors were very excited!

Mother Speranza read the first clue. "You didn't know when you came that you'd be roped into a game."

"It must be to do with the bell ropes!" they

said.

In the belltower, wrapped around one of the bell ropes, they found their next clue.

"To find the treasure you should inspect the place where the church's silver is kept."

"The treasury!" they said.

As they searched among the display cabinets with silver chalices and embroidered vestments, Silver Luce wondered if the bishop's gift might be something better than a chocolate egg.

Between the tourists milling around, they found the next clue card on the floor.

"You'll find your treasure where the foundress sleeps peacefully on a stone mattress."

"It must be by our foundress's sarcophagus!" they said.

Trying not to disturb the tour groups, they hunted around the crypt.

Searching the floor behind the Mother Foundress's sarcophagus, Sister Luce found a bunch of car keys.

They were from the same manufacturer as the bishop's minibus. The kind man must be donating the minibus to the convent!

She rushed to show them to Mother Speranza and, full of excitement, they returned to the bishop.

"We've found the keys. Thank you for your very generous gift!" Mother Speranza told him.

But he looked puzzled.

"I'm sorry but I have no idea about these keys. My present is a large egg," he said.

Then he accompanied them to the cloister where, on a rockery—the "stone mattress" of the clue—under a plant bearing the same name as their Mother Foundress, was hidden an Easter egg.

The keys, as it turned out, belonged to a visitor who had dropped them in the crypt and was looking for them.

Sister Luce felt a little disappointed. When she had had no expectation of gifts of any kind, she had been very excited at the prospect of a share in a large chocolate egg.

But since she had started expecting a minibus instead, the chocolate egg had become a disappointment. Weren't expectations the root of most unhappiness?

"I'm afraid I can't find anyone to drive you back to the convent," the bishop said. "But I have a proposal," he continued. "If you drive yourselves home in our minibus, you could keep it at the convent and share it with us until you get your own."

This wasn't the same as receiving the minibus as a gift, as Sister Luce had imagined, but it was still an excellent outcome. If she hadn't been expecting anything at all, she would have been very pleased with the arrangement, she thought to herself.

Mother Speranza accepted the offer gratefully and Sister Deodata, who drove the convent's tractor, gladly volunteered to drive everyone home.

With the huge egg in her arms, Mother Speranza sat in the minibus with a smile.

As she sat next to her, Sister Luce thought that her Mother Superior must be unaffected by the negative power of expectations.

"I'm very pleased," Mother Speranza confided to her, as they were driving along. "You see, the Easter egg and the use of the minibus are only half the bishop's gift. In order to coordinate using the minibus, the bishop and I have shared our calendars. This means that, when we need him in future, we'll be able to see if he's free and he won't be able to refuse us!"

Sister Luce chuckled. That was indeed an unexpected bonus!

## 26. SANGRIA

Now that they had the use of a minibus, Mother Speranza could start accepting invitations from neighbouring convents. Today they had been invited to attend the ceremony in which three young women would take their vows and enter the convent of the Capuchin sisters.

The ceremony was beautiful and touching, full of cheerful African songs, and was followed by an equally cheerful party on the convent's terrace.

The Capuchin sisters had prepared a feast of food from the countries of origin of their three new sisters. There were dishes that Sister Luce had never seen, smelt or tasted before, and musical instruments with exotic sounds.

Soon a conga was snaking around the terrace, picking up more people as it moved along.

Sister Luce's feet were itching to join but she

felt too shy. So she just hovered by the refreshments table, trying to look busy.

"Would you like some?" one of the Capuchin sisters asked Sister Luce.

She was serving a beautiful pink juice from out of a hollowed-out watermelon. It looked very refreshing. Sister Luce accepted it gratefully.

It tasted as good as it looked and it gave her something to hold in her hands.

The music changed and everyone began to sing "Oh Happy Day" and dancing to it. This was one of Sister Luce's favourite songs. She had to join in!

She gathered her courage and joined in with the other singing and dancing nuns. By the end of the party, Sister Luce had been singing and dancing non-stop.

That must be why her legs felt weak and her head was hurting, she thought as she struggled to climb into the minibus.

But even after supper, the headache didn't stop.

"I don't know why I've been feeling so unwell after the party," Sister Luce said to Sister Angelica, the convent's first aider.

"Maybe the sangria?"

"What sangria?"

Sister Luce learnt that what she had believed

to be watermelon juice contained a little alcohol, too. As she was a non-drinker, it had gone straight to her head.

Then she suddenly remembered something that had happened at the party. Intrigued by the drums, she had asked to have a go. She had played so enthusiastically that one of the Capuchin sisters had asked if she'd like to play with them for an event.

Sister Luce had agreed but now, in the cold light of sobriety, she regretted it. All she could hope for was that the sister who had asked her would forget.

But the following day, Mother Speranza approached her.

"I've had a call from the Capuchin sisters. They said you've agreed to play the drums with them next week," the Mother Superior said with a puzzled look.

Sister Luce wished she could say that it wasn't true. Instead, she nodded.

"I'm very pleased. Since I've thrust the documentary upon you, you've really come out of your shell." Mother Speranza smiled.

So this was why Mother Speranza had chosen her for the documentary! It was nothing to do with being photogenic. The mother superior had wanted to help her conquer her shyness!

Alas, the improvement Mother Speranza was so pleased about had only been the effect of the sangria. Sister Luce would have to make it become real.

"Alessia and Leonia will be delighted. Of course, they, too, will want to film you."

Why had the mother said "too"?

"Who else will be filming?" Sister Luce asked with trepidation.

"The national news channel, of course."

A cold shiver ran down Sister Luce's back. What event had she signed up for?

Mother Speranza looked at her. "You do know that they're taking part in Sanremo's Music Festival, don't you?"

Sister Luce would have crumpled to the floor if Mother Speranza hadn't caught her with a chair.

She had agreed to take part in the most famous music competition in the country.

"It's not too late to backtrack," Mother Speranza put in.

But this was Sister Luce's chance to conquer her shyness without sangria.

"No. I will do it."

## 27. SANREMO

Sister Luce had never seen such bright lights indoors. To be fair, she wasn't sure that a stage so big counted as indoors. Rather, it seemed to be a world of its own.

She wasn't worried about the music. Her drumming routine was simple and she had practised it to death. For the whole of last week, Mother Speranza had relieved her from every other duty so that she could practise.

But Sister Luce was worried about the stage. At the dress rehearsal it had felt enormous and intimidating. Today, at the real thing, an entire theatre full of people would be watching her and the other nuns perform up on that stage.

Not that the other sisters seemed to mind: even the ones who would be singing and playing in the front row looked excited rather than frozen in fear.

Sister Pascal, the band leader, led a prayer. They all joined hands in a circle and closed their eyes, backstage.

As they got ready to move to the stage, someone ran towards them.

"Stop! The order of the songs has been changed! You don't go onstage for another hour," the woman with the clipboard told them.

Oh, no! Now Sister Luce would have to panic all over again in one hour's time!

"While you're waiting for your slot, we have an interview ready for you," the woman continued.

This was even worse! Sister Luce would have much rather be left alone in a dark corner for an hour.

But interviews were important. It was there that they could talk about their vocation. So she followed the others to the interview corner.

The place was tiny, clearly designed for smaller groups than the sisters' fifteen-strong band. Sister Luce took the chance to hide at the back and discreetly slip behind the board. Taking up her rosary chain in her hands, she closed her eyes and began to pray.

From the other side of the board, she could hear Sister Pascal answer the interviewer's questions.

"When our drummer injured her wrists and she couldn't play anymore, we simply didn't know what to do. But we prayed hard and we were sent Sister Luce!"

At the mention of her name, Sister Luce jumped and almost dropped her rosary chain.

"Where is she?" the interviewer asked.

Sister Luce didn't have time to decide if she should come out of hiding or she should hide better. Next thing she knew, a camera had found her and she was being filmed then and there.

"And there she is, the one who saved the day—praying, like all nuns do," the interviewer said to the camera.

The chatty interviewer proceeded to ask Sister Luce some questions, which she answered in monosyllables.

By the time that ordeal was over, Sister Luce was looking forward to walking onto the stage and having it all over and done with.

When they were called up on stage, she bounced in, undaunted by the lights or the applause. She was a woman on a mission.

She played the drums with unprecedented energy and got so deeply into the music that she forgot the audience, the cameras and even the judges. She was having fun!

When their piece was over and the audience erupted into applause, Sister Luce smiled and bowed like the others, undaunted by the attention.

Maybe, she thought to herself, she had finally conquered her shyness!

Shy moments would surely come to her again—shyness was in her nature, and she would always have to live with it. But if it didn't stop her doing the things she wanted to do anymore, she would be more than happy.

Of course, she hadn't done it all on her own. Situations and people—and God—had challenged and helped her in that journey. But she could be pleased with herself too.

So, as the audience continued to clap, she bowed again, imagining that they were cheering her victory over shyness.

## 28. MOTHER'S HEN

Sister Luce and the four guests were sitting in the garden in bloom.

"Next Sunday will be Mother's Day!" Alba suddenly said.

Was it already the second Sunday in May? Sister Luce felt that time had flown since the four women had come to the convent.

"This Mother's Day will be hard for Sister Grazia," Sister Luce said ruefully.

"Why? Is she sad because she'll never be a mum?" Giorgia asked.

"No. Her mother has just passed away in the Philippines and Sister Grazia wasn't able to see her before she died."

"Poor Sister Grazia," Alba said. "What about you, Sister Luce? Are you ever sad you'll never have children of your own?"

"No. When your heart is full of God's love, you don't miss anything," Sister Luce replied candidly.

Then the conversation moved back to Sister Grazia and on how they could make this Mother's Day a little less sad for her.

After all that talking of mothers, Sister Luce decided to ring her own mother for some early Mother's Day wishes.

"I'm happy you rang today. This morning I met the mother of your friend Adriana. She told me that her daughter is expecting a baby," her mum told her.

Sister Luce felt the flagstones shift under her sandals. Adriana had been in her class at school and was the same age as her. If Adriana was old enough to start a family, Sister Luce must be too!

Giving up motherhood hadn't felt like a big sacrifice while Sister Luce felt she was too young for it anyway. But now that her peers were starting families, she would soon feel left behind!

It dawned on Sister Luce that, being an only child, she was her mother's only chance to have grandchildren. So her mother would never have any.

With these thoughts in her mind, Sister Luce went to sleep a little sad that night.

The next morning, when Sister Luce was feeding her hens, Sister Grazia walked past the chicken coop and stopped.

"My mother used to pet our hens just like you do, and we used to call her Mother Hen," Sister Grazia said. "You remind me so much of her that, from now on, I'll call you Mother Hen. You'll be Mother Hen for me even if you become Mother Superior."

Sister Luce chuckled. "That's the only mother I will ever be," she said.

"That's not true," Sister Grazia said. "Maybe you won't be a Mother Superior, but you are already a mother to all the people you look after. Being a mother means giving life and helping others grow and thrive."

Sister Luce thought about it. Sister Grazia was right. There were many other ways to be life-givers than giving birth.

A black hen pulled at her skirt because she had stopped scattering the seeds.

"I know, I know," Sister Luce said, resuming her job.

"This hen looks just like my mother's favourite," Sister Grazia said, petting the bird on the head.

As she watched Sister Grazia head off to the pilgrims' guesthouse, Sister Luce had an idea.

On Mother's Day, Sister Luce and the others handed Sister Grazia a wicker basket tied with a pretty ribbon.

"A present for me? Why?"

"To cheer you up," Alba said,

"We thought that today you might be a little down because of your loss," Dina explained.

"That's a very kind thought, thank you," Sister Grazia said. "But I'm not sad. I miss my mum, but when she was still in this world, she was in the Philippines and we were thousands of miles apart. Now that she's with Jesus, instead, we're much closer. But I still love presents," Sister Grazia said with a childish grin, and pulled the ribbon of the basket.

A cheeky black hen jumped out of the basket, clucking loudly.

"My mum's favourite hen's lookalike!" Sister Grazia said excitedly.

"We thought you might like to keep her with you at the pilgrims' guesthouse," Sister Luce said.

"I'd love to! But I don't deserve such a good present."

"Yes, you do," Sister Luce said. "Today is Mother's Day and, as you taught me, we're all mothers if we are life-givers—which you definitely are."

Sister Grazia scooped the hen in her arms. "Thank you."

## 29. PARTING GIFTS

The documentary was coming to an end. Only a few months earlier, Sister Luce had been looking forward to this moment. Now, instead, she felt a pang of sadness.

She had grown fond of the guests, the producer and the camerawoman, and she was going to miss them. No doubt, the entire convent was going to miss them.

Sister Luce thought that the occasion required a proper send-off, so she asked Mother Speranza if they could give them a goodbye party and some parting gifts.

"That's an excellent idea. I'll ask Sister Veronica to prepare a special dinner. As for the gifts, we could give them a chestnut cake from our grove and a bottle of wine each," the Mother suggested.

They were perfectly suitable presents, but Sister Luce wasn't satisfied.

"I was thinking of a keepsake to remember

their time here," she said.

Mother Speranza agreed that this was a better idea, and left Sister Luce in charge of choosing suitable gifts.

Sister Luce set off on a brainstorming stroll.

She came across Sister Silvestra transporting some wood. She was carrying some beautiful cross-section slices of a chestnut tree they had felled last winter. Surely something nice could be made out of them!

"Can I have six?" Sister Luce asked. "I'd like to make a parting gift for our guests."

"Sure!" Sister Silvestra replied gladly. "Sister Benedetta will have everything you need in her woodworking workshop."

Sister Luce was delighted when Sister Benedetta gave her the convent's new pyrography pen and some hooks to hang the slices like pictures!

Sister Luce decided to write a different Bible quote on every slice.

For Alessia, the producer, who never took any rest, she wrote, *On the seventh day, God rested from all his work.*

For Giorgia, who loved nature, she wrote, *God created the heavens and the earth.*

For Dina, who had recently made peace with her sibling, she quoted a Psalm: *How wonderful and delightful it is for brothers to live together in unity.*

Each of the six women had her own quote especially chosen by Sister Luce.

Sister Luce was just finishing writing on the last slice when the bell rang for the Angelus. She stopped her work and joined the others in the chapel.

But as she sang the last notes, a doubt came into her mind. Had she turned the pyrographer off?

While the other sisters filed out of the chapel in an orderly queue, Sister Luce hitched up her skirt and ran back to the workshop as fast as she could.

A smell of burning gave her the answer she didn't want.

Thankfully the fire hadn't spread beyond the workbench and, with a couple of bucketfuls of water, she managed to extinguish it. But the wood slices were charred and sooty, and Sister Luce's quotes were completely illegible.

Now the only Biblical message these burnt wood slices conveyed was "ashes to ashes".

"Don't despair, Sister Luce," Sister Benedetta told her. "I've got a marvellous sander. Never despair."

The two nuns got to work and, a few hours later, the wood slices had a clean surface for Sister Luce to write on all over again. This time, having practised before, she wrote with an even neater hand.

On the day of the goodbye party, unfortunately, there was one absence. Alessia had had to dash off to another project. The Bible quote Sister Luce had chosen for her couldn't have been more appropriate.

After Mother Speranza's speech, Sister Luce handed out the gifts to the departing women. Everyone was emotional and there were a few tears.

"You've given us beautiful parting gifts, Sister. I will hang mine the other way round," Matilde said.

"Is there another way round?" the other asked, turning their wood slices. "Oh!"

"I had a little accident with the pyrographer," Sister Luce explained.

She and Sister Benedetta had sanded the fronts of the wood but they had left the back charred. Then, on the burnt wood, Sister Luce had carved the words Sister Benedetta had told her when all had seemed lost: *Never despair.*

## 30. GIVE ME PEACE

Sister Luce couldn't bear to watch herself on a screen. The rest of the convent had gathered in the recreation room to watch the documentary on TV.

Some sisters commented about unflattering lighting and angles but, overall, everyone was pleased with the end result of all those months of filming.

They were also pleased with the minibus Mother Speranza had purchased with the documentary money. And Mother Speranza was pleased with her continued access to the bishop's calendar, despite having returned the loaned minibus to him.

But the other, more important, fruits that everyone had hoped the documentary would deliver were not yet materialising. There had been no enquiries from women interested in a life devoted to God.

Mother Speranza had spent long hours in

her office, but the only enquiries she had received were from suppliers chasing payments.

One afternoon, though, an unexpected phone call came through.

"Alessia is coming to visit us," Mother Speranza announced.

As the Mother Superior didn't know the reason for the producer's visit, they couldn't tell if it was good or bad news. The whole convent was on tenterhooks for the entire day.

When Alessia finally walked into the chapel that evening, she was unsmiling, pale and drawn.

Mother Speranza greeted her and suggested they went to her office to talk. However, Alessia said that she'd rather go to sleep and see them in the morning.

So Mother Speranza entrusted her to Sister Giovanna, who ran the guesthouse, then turned to Sister Luce.

"If Alessia is staying the night, it must be a very serious matter," she confided.

With such worries on her mind, Sister Luce slept badly and, judging by the bags under Mother Speranza's eyes, so had she.

Alessia, on the contrary, looked much better than she had the previous night.

Throughout that day, Sister Luce and

Mother Speranza waited for the producer to break whatever terrible news she had come to deliver, but Alessia never asked for a meeting.

Instead, she spent the day helping Sister Deodata in the vineyard, Sister Silvestra in the chestnut grove and Sister Veronica in the kitchen. By suppertime, it was clear that Alessia wasn't going to initiate the discussion.

"What are we to do?" Mother Speranza asked Sister Luce.

"If we start a difficult conversation so late in the day, we'll have another bad night's sleep," Sister Luce pointed out, so they decided to put the matter off to the following day.

Still, this didn't stop them having another night of fitful sleep, and the next morning, they looked as tired as Alessia had on her arrival.

She, instead, was flourishing. The bags under her eyes were gone, her skin had the healthy glow of someone who has spent time outdoors, and she had started to smile again.

Mother Speranza and Sister Luce finally cornered her in the pilgrims' guesthouse.

"Would you like to discuss the reason of your visit now?" Mother Speranza asked.

Alessia's smile drained. "It's an upsetting and unpleasant matter."

"Is there trouble?" Mother Speranza asked, blanching.

"I'm afraid yes," Alessia replied.

She then recounted how she had got herself so overworked and stressed that she had been snapping at her staff.

"I realised that I was on the verge of burnout and I immediately thought of you. This convent is so peaceful and life here is so well-balanced that I decided I had to come to you. You say your peace comes from God. I don't believe in God but I thought that, if I came here, some of your peace and happiness might rub off on me. I've been here one day and it's already working," Alessia concluded with a smile.

Sister Luce and Mother Speranza looked at each other and chuckled. If only Alessia knew how their own peace and happiness had been tested by her arrival!

## 31. SHEPHERDESSES

Alessia had departed looking much better than when she had arrived, and life in the convent had returned to normal.

Sister Luce was back with her hens and was now also in charge of a small flock of sheep, which gave her great pleasure.

The fruits of the documentary, though, weren't clear. If the Lord worked in mysterious ways, they were far too mysterious for Sister Luce to understand.

"We wanted to show the world that convent life isn't one of sadness and regret, and I think we've achieved that," Mother Speranza said during the general meeting she had called to draw a balance of the experience.

Everyone agreed.

"I know that it's the Lord's job to call people to Himself, but I thought that we could be a channel of that through the documentary. I had hoped that we might spark interest in convent life, but we haven't received any enquiries," Mother Superior added despondently.

"Actually, we have," Sister Giovanna said, to everyone's surprise. "Not from women interested in becoming nuns, but from people eager to join us for a while. The bookings for the pilgrims' guesthouse have rocketed," she explained.

Sister Giovanna reminded them that, before the documentary, the guesthouse had mostly hosted people on walking routes to St Francis's pilgrimage places.

"The guests who have been coming recently are different. They come to experience the peace of our convent."

Sister Giovanna had included, *What do you hope to gain from your stay?* in the welcome questionnaire. And some people had written "making important decisions", "finding myself" and "finding God". It was clear that they were looking for more than board and lodging.

"These guests need us to inspire and encourage them," Mother Speranza said.

"Sister Grazia and I are rushed off our feet with a full house every day," Sister Giovanna said apologetically.

"We don't expect you to do this job too.

You're already running the house and we shall give you help with that too," Mother Speranza said, and turned to Sister Luce.

A frisson ran down Sister Luce's back. Goodbye hens and sheep, she thought. From now on, she would be preparing breakfasts, stripping beds and cleaning rooms, working indoors all the time.

"Sister Luce, would you like to help?" Mother Speranza asked her, just as she had dreaded.

A few months ago, Sister Luce would have agreed without a comment.

"I would prefer to work outdoors, but I will do whatever is needed," she said instead.

"You can certainly work outdoors," Mother Speranza said with a smile.

Sister Luce was confused. Was her Mother Superior asking her to wash the guesthouse's dirty linen on the riverbed's stones?

"Yes, you could take the guests on one-to-one walks, where they can talk about themselves, and you can listen and offer wisdom and guidance. You will help them find themselves and God in nature."

It did sound like a wonderful job.

"But I don't think I'm wise enough," Sister Luce replied.

"Don't worry. God will give you the right

words when you need them."

"But what about helping Sister Giovanna and Sister Grazia in the guesthouse? Who will change the beds, clean the rooms, prepare breakfast, welcome the guests?"

Mother Speranza smiled. "As it happens, I have already received two job applications and, by the sound of things, there will be enough work to employ both applicants. One person could help Sister Giovanna and Sister Grazia in the guesthouse, while the other could be shared between the guesthouse and the hens and the sheep."

Sister Luce imagined having to work with a stranger. Were they going to get on well together?

"Don't look so sad," Mother Speranza said. "I'm sure you will love working with Giorgia. And the other applicant is Alba. They've asked to come back to stay."

This was excellent news and everyone cheered, beginning with Sister Luce.

She was beginning to understand the Lord's mysterious ways just a little bit better.

The End

## Other books in this series:

### Tales from the Parish

Father Okoli dreams of owning a flock of hens and studying for a PhD, when his bishop saddles him with yet another parish to look after. But as Father moves to Moreton-on-the-Edge, a farming village in the English Cotswolds, he's plugged into a community of warm-hearted characters, from the motherly parish secretary to her septuagenarian neighbour who's become a cycling champion, and from teenagers requiring driving lessons to atheist publicans who believe in miracles.

Between a wacky race and a scarecrow competition, a village fête and a mop fair, Father foils cattle rustlers, fends off foxes and goes viral on the internet. As the community pulls together to reopen the village's Electric Picture House, dreams are fulfilled, teen love blossoms and Father Okoli feels that Moreton-on-the-Edge is now home.

### Welcome to Quayside

Forty-year-old Tanya Baker dreams of starting a new life and making friends when she moves to a block of flats by the River Thames with her thirteen-year-old daughter, Hattie. But as Tanya and Hattie knock on neighbours' doors in search of a tin opener, it's clear that the residents of Number One Quayside like to keep to themselves. Everyone, that is, except their next-door neighbours, Italian chef Giacomo Dalamo, and his thirteen-year-old daughter, Frankie. Between a delicious dish of lasagne (Giacomo's) and a burnt salad (Tanya's), they hatch a plan to set up a library of things in their building, so that residents can borrow rarely-used items, from DIY tools to sports equipment and party supplies. As all the residents at Quayside pull together to make the library happen, dreams are fulfilled, a community is born and love blossoms again.

**Other books by Stefania Hartley**

**Cosy mysteries:**

**Father Roberto and The Missing Money**

**Father Roberto and the Runaway Ring**

**Father Roberto and the Rural Riots**

## Short stories collections:

### Keeping it Cool

Every good mum knows how to keep her daughter safe. But how will Izzy's mum cope on a visit to a perilous ice rink? Josh thinks Elise's boyfriend wish list is rather unusual. Can he tick all the boxes? Mario knows that his name is as common in Italy as John Smith. But why are his friends sending him funeral wreaths? Ten humorous and uplifting stories, perfect for your coffee break.

### Sand, Sea & Tamburello

When Rosetta dries her hair on her balcony, she's not interested in the sun's warmth but in the young fishmonger who's eager to warm her heart. Can Don Pericle be a gracious host when an entire wedding party gets stranded at his villa? Tanino and Melina have a tough job competing with Valentina's other grandparents who take her on exhilarating trips to the beach. What can Alfonso do when his neighbours' karaoke parties become too much?

Ten stories that sparkle with the Sicilian sea, ring with the singsongs of fishmongers, and warm the heart like the summer's sun.

### To Be Loved
Amanda's name means "to be loved" and she's taken it as her duty to make herself lovable, but it's hard work. Has Tanino really abandoned Melina to freeze at home? Mark hasn't seen Nora for thirty years and, since then, he's lost a leg and all his hair. If he wasn't enough for her then, how can he be now? What happens if the dating app's algorithms go haywire?

### Drive Me Crazy
"Cohabitation is tribulation" goes an Italian saying, and after more than fifty years of married life, Tanino and Melina know a thing or two about the challenges of living together.

### Stars Are Silver
Is it too late for Melina to learn to drive? Is Don Pericle's vow never to fall in love again still valid after fifty years? Will a falling piano squash Filomena or just shake up her heart? Why does the mother of the bride ask Don Pericle to cancel the wedding?

### Fresh from the Sea
Will Gnà Peppina give her customers what they need, even if it's more than food? What

pleasures can a man indulge in after his wife has put him on a draconian diet? Who will be able to cook dinner for the family with five euros?

### Confetti and Lemon Blossom

For Don Pericle, wedding organising is a calling, not just a career. Deep in the Sicilian countryside, between rose gardens and trellised balconies, up marble staircases and across damasked ballrooms, these charming stories unfold: stories of star-crossed love, of comedic misunderstandings and of deep friendships, of love triumphing in the face of adversity.

### A Slip of the Tongue

Will Melina regret faking to be sick to avoid her chores? Can Don Pericle organise a wedding for a groom who doesn't know? Who has stolen the marble pisces from the cathedral's floor?

### What's Yours is Mine

Can Melina give away her husband's possessions because they've always said that 'what's mine is yours and what's yours is mine'? Will the 'Sleep Doctor' deliver on his promises? How will the young Sicilian duke,

Pericle, help his friend get married?

## A Season of Goodwill

How far should Viviana's family go to avoid being thirteen at the table? Should Melina and Tanino attend a New Year's party hosted by Melina's old flame? Why do Don Pericle's clients want a Christmas wedding at all costs?

## Romance novellas:

## How to Choose a Husband

Grazia Colonna has waited fifty years to meet The One. Now that her best friend is getting married for the second time, Grazia is sure that she'll meet The One at Rebecca's wedding. He will sweep Grazia off her feet and snatch her from the clutches of her bullying mother.

But first Grazia needs to alter the dress she will wear at the event and, for this, she needs the help of the village's grumpy widower tailor, Hector Gonzales.

As the bride is stuck abroad and may not get back in time for the wedding, Grazia and Hector are forced to work together and, inconveniently, they fall in love.

Can they ensure that the right wedding

goes ahead and the wrong one doesn't?

**The Italian Fake Date**
When Alice Baker discovers that she's been adopted, she knows she won't have peace until she's found her Italian birth mother. But all she has is a letter written twenty-five years ago and an old address.
Jaded about love and unable to forgive his ex-fiancée and his brother, Paolo Rondino is struggling to find inspiration for a sculpture that will make or break his career. Hoping that a trip home will help him find his muse again, he decides to return to Italy, even if this means confronting the two people who betrayed him.
Alice and Paolo strike a deal: he will help her find her birth mother and she will pretend to be his girlfriend to please his mother. It looks like the perfect exchange, until real feelings start to grow…

**Sweet Competition for Camillo's Café**
Camillo runs a popular café on Altavicia's main square. Giada runs an equally popular café across the square. They have both entered Altavicia's Best Café competition.
Scarred by his father's death, Camillo's greatest wish is to escape the Calabrian seaside

village and return to his beloved London, where his family was last together and happy. Abandoned by her parents, Giada's greatest wish is to earn her nonna's love. The competition trophy is the ticket to both their dreams, but only one can win.

As Camillo discovers that happiness doesn't come from a location and Giada that love isn't earned, can enemies become friends, and maybe more?

**Second Chances at Mamma's Trattoria**

When Eleonora got a job at Mamma Cristina's trattoria, she didn't tell the sweet old woman that she was her son's ex-wife, nor that the twins are her granddaughters. Her plan was to give the twins a taste of family life without any of the trouble. But she had not planned for Davide to come home.

Davide loves his job at sea and he wouldn't have come home if it hadn't been for Mamma Cristina's health scare. The last thing he expected to find was his ex-wife implanted in the heart of his home with two young daughters in tow.

The last thing Eleonora and Davide want is to work together. But a celebrity Christmas wedding at the trattoria requires every hand on deck.

How long can Eleonora and Davide avoid each other while working together and living under the same roof?

**Under Far Eastern Skies**

Everyone thinks that thirty-one-year-old Shona Wells should get married: her overbearing father, her starry-eyed little sister, and the whole expat community in 1930s Singapore. But Shona wants independence and the freedom to choose her own way, to travel the world exploring nature.

The last thing twenty-five-year old Will Palmer needs is marriage. He's too busy discovering new plant species in the remotest jungles in the world.

But then, three days before Shona is due to sail back to England, she meets Will, and finds someone with the same passion for the natural world. They are perfect for each other, until a series of misadventures and misunderstandings threatens to pull them apart forever.

## ABOUT THE AUTHOR

Stefania was born in Sicily and immediately started growing, but not very much. She left her sunny island after falling head over heels in love with an Englishman, and now she lives in the UK with her husband and their three children. Having finally learnt English, she's enjoying it so much that she now writes novels and short stories which have been longlisted, shortlisted, commended, and won prizes.

She'd love you to leave a review and to sign up for her newsletter so she can let you know when a new book is out:

www.stefaniahartley.com/subscribe

You'll also receive an exclusive short story.

Printed in Dunstable, United Kingdom